OUT OF THE BURROW

Out of the Burrow

FOUR STORIES

Kennett Lehmann

••••

STORIES

ACKNOWLEDGMENTS

For much appreciated advice and help, the author would like to thank Phoebe Love, Maddy Oberman, Paul Lehmann, Jack Lehmann, and René Spencer Saller.

Having a Car at College

WEAR MARKS

It was midmorning on the second Saturday of fall term, and Myra, a nineteen-year-old freshman from Kansas City, was driving east on Broadway in downtown Columbia looking for wear marks.

Her one idea had been to inspect the line of drive-up mailboxes outside the post office. She had hoped to find that the mailbox first in line would show some slight abrasion of the paint around the slot indicating that it was the mailbox most often used. This preference could then be interpreted as a function of the hectic pace of modern life (or something like that), wherein people felt compelled to relieve themselves of their outgoing letters at the first possible opportunity. But when she entered the drive-up in her sporty little two-seater and lowered the window, she could detect no wear mark distinguishing any of the boxes. They all looked spanking new.

Now she was back on Broadway trying to find something else. Approaching the City Hall building at Broadway and Seventh, she saw what looked like a filled-in pothole in the left-turn lane. This surely was a wear mark. But how to interpret it? Myra could think of no reason why there should be more drivers wanting to turn left at Seventh than to go straight or to turn right.

She noticed that the street surface had cracks in the paving. The cracks were more or less all over. Could anything interesting or unusual be interpreted about that?

At Broadway and Eighth there was a restaurant with a brown awning in front that was discolored by some sort of residue. You could see that something was seeping out from between the white masonry tiles above that left black streaks as it dribbled down. Clearly, the discoloration on the awning was a function of the seeping—

Myra let it go by. She crossed Eighth, then Ninth, then Tenth. When she got to Hitt Street, she made a right turn and then another right to get onto Cherry. Coming down that street, she spotted a parking space by the side of the coffee shop on the corner at Ninth. She slid her vehicle into the space, got out, and went into the shop and ordered herself a cup of plain black coffee at the counter.

"Make it the largest size, please!"

After she had been served, she sat down at a table and got out her phone. There was a text message from Cecile, one of her classmates.

Cecile wanted to know what, if anything, Myra had found for the wear-mark assignment.

"Nothing," Myra texted back.

Cecile's reply came almost immediately.

"We should join forces!"

"We should!" Myra texted.

"Can you pick me up?" Cecile didn't have a car.

Myra drove onto campus and picked her up outside of Atchison, one of the high-rise residence halls built during the 1950s that hadn't been demolished yet.

As soon as Cecile got in the car, she said, "OK, let's go!"

"Where?" said Myra.

"I don't know."

They left campus and, once more, Myra headed towards Broadway. She told Cecile about her unsuccessful attempt to find wear marks at the drive-up boxes outside the post office.

"That's too bad!" said Cecile. "It was a good idea, especially the interpretation."

"I know!"

"Don't worry. We'll find something."

When they got to Broadway, Myra turned west, away from downtown. She wanted to look someplace new, so she and Cecile decided they would go to Columbia Mall. Three blocks on, they stopped for a red light.

"What about *that* place?" said Cecile. She was looking at the building on the southwest corner of the intersection. This wasn't the first time Cecile had noticed it—she had come this way before—but she hadn't connected it with any particular function. The building was conspicuous for its long, curved front and irregularly ("whimsically") positioned windows and an outsized glass-brick entrance pavilion in the shape of a sawed-off cone. Most conspicuous of all was a tall, bright-yellow metal sculpture of protruding spars and spikes that stood by the door, as though guarding it.

Myra spotted an identifying lamppost banner.

"It's the library."

Cecile, whose grandmother was a retired middle-school librarian, was getting an idea.

"Let's go inside. Turn!"

They weren't in the left-turn lane. That lane was occupied by the car next to them, waiting for the arrow.

"I'll have to go straight and then come back."

"Cut in front of the guy!" said Cecile, meaning the car next to them.

Myra put her blinker on and eased the car forward and partway over. This maneuver resulted in an angry blast of the horn from the other car.

The light was still red, but there was no cross traffic. Myra went ahead and completed the turn.

"I hope there are no cops around!" said Cecile.

Myra turned into the big lot behind the building.

"We need to look inside the books!" Cecile explained. "The dates that are stamped on the due-date slips—they're *wear marks*."

Myra parked the car and switched the engine off. She was a little rattled.

"The dates—"

"They're a sign the books are being *used*," continued Cecile, "that they're being checked out. We just look inside the front covers."

"So then—what?"

"So then we see how many stamps there are. A *lot* of stamps on the slip means the book's been checked out a *lot* of times. Or at least renewed a lot of times. That's how we know the book is popular."

"And then?"

"And then that's it. We say that the number of stamps on the due-date slip is a *function* of how popular the book is with the reading public."

"That's the interpretation?"

"All we need to do is look at something like *Harry Potter* and then compare it with some clunker no one likes."

When they got inside the building, Myra and Cecile went up to the second floor where the fiction stacks were located. Myra pulled out a random hardback and opened the front cover. There was no due-date slip pasted inside.

"This one doesn't have anything," she said. She showed Cecile the blank front endpapers.

"What about in the back?"

Myra flipped the pages. There was nothing inside the back cover either.

Myra reshelved the book. Cecile started pulling out books one after the other, examining the inside front and back covers of each one and reshelving it before going on to the next. An old man with a yellow beard came by and stopped at the end of the stack to watch. He was holding a newspaper in his hand.

"Don't they *use* them anymore?" Cecile said with a frown.

"At Ingleglade they just printed out a loose slip. They didn't stamp anything inside the book." Myra was referring to the check-out routine at the library of her high school. "After they scanned it."

"Oh!" Cecile blushed. She hadn't checked a book out of a library in a very long time. Her memory of pasted-in due-date slips was based on a number of old library discards that had been passed on to her mother by her grandmother back in the '70s when her mother was a girl. "Well, crap!"

Myra thought for a moment.

"What about pages that are dog-eared? That would count as a wear mark, wouldn't it?"

"I guess."

The old man holding the newspaper was grinning at them.

"Are you two *sisters?*" he said.

Myra gave him a smile and shook her head.

"Let's go to a different section," said Cecile.

They moved away.

"As if *we* could be sisters!" Cecile commented. Myra was tall and slender and had dusky skin and long, luxuriant dark-blond hair. She was beautiful. Cecile was shorter, busty, and somewhat heavyset. Her complexion was like a redhead's, though her hair, which she wore short, was more brown than red. She was not unattractive, but, unlike Myra, she took no pains with her appearance. Where Myra always dressed well, whether formally or informally, Cecile never put on anything more stylish than an oversized T-shirt or sweatshirt.

"Biography!" said Myra. They had wandered into the biography section. Myra took a volume off the shelf and started leafing through it. "This one's all marked up!"

"Marked up how?" said Cecile.

"Underlines and stuff."

"Lemme see!"

Myra showed her one of the pages. In the margin, someone had written, in pen, *This is such an exaggeration.* The comment referred to an underlined passage of text that read,

> Mauriac proved to be a frail, intense man of a kind often found among French writers and intellectuals, who seem to shake themselves to pieces with the vigour and urgency of their thoughts and words; like some ancient rickety old car which shakes and shivers when the en-

gine is started up, so that one constantly marvels that it can hold together at all.

With Myra still holding on to the book, Cecile carefully flipped the pages to the title page. The title of the book was *Chronicles of Wasted Time*. It was by Malcolm Muggeridge.

"Huh!" she said and flipped the pages back.

"The comment is a wear mark, right?" said Myra.

"Sure."

"And it indicates the sociological context, right? Which is that the guy who wrote the comment wants to say what he thinks about what the author wrote. That he *questions* the author's view of—" Myra read the passage over. "Mauriac and the French writers and intellectuals."

"But that's only because that's what the comment *says*, what the guy *wrote*."

"Yeah, so?"

"I mean," said Cecile, "it's not like it's a sign of something else, something that we have to figure out, like the guy was a Republican or something."

Myra looked at the facing page. There, a large exclamation point had been drawn next to a passage that read,

Nothing impresses the English more than to live to a ripe old age, something that sufficed to make even so ill-tempered an old lady as Queen Victoria popular.

"I don't like this assignment," Myra said.

"Let's get out of here," said Cecile.

Myra reshelved the book, and the two left the library.

They proceeded on to Columbia Mall. Myra found a parking space close to the mall entrance. First she overshot it, then put the car in reverse, then parked head on. She and Cecile got out of the car.

Cecile surveyed the huge lot.

"Did you see the oil stain?"

"What oil stain?" said Myra.

"On our parking space!" Cecile went to the back of the car and waited for a pickup truck to go by. Then, with the lane clear, she got down on her hands and knees. "Dang it! Can't see it now." She stood up and walked along the row of parked cars in the direction away from the mall entrance till she came to an empty space. "Look at this!"

Myra came up and looked. There was an oil stain at the far end of the space.

"This oil stain isn't as big as the one on our space," said Cecile. "Not nearly. This tells us that the *farther* away a parking space is from the entrance to the mall, the *less* it's used compared with the closer spaces. Look!" She pointed to a remote part of the lot where there were hardly any cars parked. "No oil stains. Clean as a whistle."

"Huh!" said Myra. "But can't we tell just by looking at where the cars are parked that people want to park as close to the mall entrance as possible?"

"That's not our problem. We're just supposed to be looking for wear marks." Cecile took a picture of the oil stain with her phone. "Besides, if we came out here at three o'clock in the morning on Christmas Eve when there weren't any cars on the lot at all, we'd only have the oil stains to go by. And they would tell the story!"

It didn't seem to Myra like a very profound interpretation. But the assignment didn't say anything about having to be profound.

"We can't both use the oil stains," she said. "You saw them first. I'll have to keep looking."

"Don't worry. We'll find something."

They went into the mall. Cecile wanted to get something to eat. At the food court she ordered a deluxe platter from the taco counter. Myra, who tried to watch what she ate, ordered a salad. After they were served, they found a table and sat down with their trays.

"We just need to brainstorm," said Cecile. She took a bite of her burrito and began to chew. "But we need to bring in reinforcements. We need to talk to Hayden."

"Who's Hayden?"

"He's my go-to guy. He lives in West."

"Hayden would be a good person to talk to about wear marks?"

"He'll have some ideas. He knows a lot."

Cecile got out her phone and began to text.

After a minute or two, she said, "Can we stop by Atchison and get my laundry?"

"You need to do laundry?"

"Hayden says I can bring it to West. We can kill two birds with one stone."

"All right."

"The facilities in Atchison suck!"

When they were finished with their lunch, they drove to one of the remote student parking lots on campus and then walked to Atchison, where Cecile picked up her laundry hamper and a jug of detergent. Myra took charge of the jug of detergent, and they continued on foot to West, one of three newer residence halls that had been built just across the lane from the high-rise block Atchison was part of. Hayden had told Cecile to come to a side door. At the door, Cecile put the hamper down and texted Hayden that she and Myra were outside ready to be let in.

"You wanna go to Shakespeare's tonight?" Cecile asked Myra.

Myra liked pizza, but she didn't want to think about going out.

"I need to get this assignment done. I also have about a million pages for English."

"Get the Cliff Notes!"

"She gave us this article on theory that's impossible to understand. It's all gobbledygook."

"Skip it."

"I'm going to change my major to Spanish." Myra had taken both AP English and AP Spanish in high school but hadn't declared for anything yet. She had been leaning towards English. She liked reading novels, especially the Victorian classics, but she didn't like reading theory, even when she could understand it. Cecile, who didn't like reading much of anything (despite having an ex-librarian grandmother), was intending to major in something practical, like food science and nutrition.

The expressionless face of a youth appeared in the window of the security door.

"Hey!" said Cecile in her heartiest manner.

Hayden pushed the door open.

Cecile picked up the laundry hamper.

"Hayden, this is Myra, who I told you about."

"Come in," said Hayden. He stepped back inside the building.

"Hi," said Myra.

Hayden led them to the laundry room.

"The promised land!" said Cecile as they entered the facility. "Now Hayden, don't go away, 'cause we need to talk."

"OK." Hayden had yet to crack a smile.

They had the room to themselves, and Cecile chose a washer in the center of the bank of machines.

"Just lemme get these clothes started." She put the hamper down. "Detergent please!" Myra handed her the bright orange jug.

Hayden looked at Myra and raised an eyebrow. Myra just smiled. Whenever she met a man, she automatically assigned him to one of two categories: Potentially Eligible or Definitely Not Eligible. Hayden, who hadn't yet fully grown into his tall frame, fell into the latter category. Hayden himself knew that he fell into this category—he knew it before Myra did, when he saw her face through the window of the security door. The raised eyebrow was an invitation to Myra to contemplate the bossy behavior of their mutual friend Cecile.

"All right," said Cecile when she had gotten the washer going.

She proceeded to explain to Hayden the wear-mark assignment. It was for one of the classes she and Myra were taking together, People, Habitat, and Nature, and it was due in class Monday. Each student was to seek out a *wear mark*, or a pattern of wear marks, take a picture of it, and write up a report on it. The wear mark could be large or small, indoors or out, on campus or off. The only requirement was that it be "created by humans" and be of a material nature (not virtual or electronic). The student was to interpret the wear mark in terms of the social and/or environmental context in which it occurred. Cecile related her and Myra's adventures at the public library and at the parking lot at Columbia Mall, where she, Cecile, had found the oil stains. But she and Myra couldn't both use the oil stains.

"You gotta think of a wear mark for Myra!" Cecile concluded.

Hayden considered the problem.

"What about something in Atchison?" he said.

Cecile groaned.

"I don't want to look in *Atch*ison!"

"It's a pretty old building. Something in the laundry room—"

"No! I hate that place."

"What about Blitzing?" He said to Myra, "We should go over to Blitzing. That place is full of wear marks."

"What's Blitzing?" said Myra.

"Blitzing Hall. You don't have any classes in Blitzing? You're lucky."

Blitzing Hall was a glass-box creation from the 1960s, constructed according to precise, state-of-the-art engineering specifications. There had been no "overbuilding." The result was that, fifty years later, the building was coming apart at the seams and people hated taking classes there.

"They oughta tear it down," said Hayden critically. "Shall we go on over?"

"I can't go *now*," said Cecile. "I gotta tend to this laundry!"

"Myra and I can go." Hayden was wearing a deadpan expression.

The washing machine was making its normal, high-efficiency noises.

Myra said to Cecile, "Can't you leave the washer going? You can put the clothes in the dryer when we get back."

"I can't leave my laundry! Somebody might steal it."

"No one's gonna steal your *laundry*," said Hayden.

"Somebody might steal my hamper."

Hayden knew all about the hamper. He had driven Cecile to Target at Columbia Mall to get it. It was made of real wickerwork.

"You don't want to go over later?" said Cecile.

"I'd rather get it done now," said Myra.

"Wait—I have an idea! Why don't *you* take the oil stains for your wear mark, and *I'll* go with Hayden to Blitzing later and get something else. That way you can get started writing up the interpretation."

This seemed like a very kind offer on Cecile's part.

"Aw—I couldn't let you do that!" said Myra. She said to Hayden, "Let's go to Blitzing!"

* * *

Hayden and Myra started off across campus.

"How did you get to be friends with Cecile?" Hayden asked as they walked along.

"We're taking Intro to Geology together—in addition to People, Habitat, and Nature, the class we need the wear marks for."

"Do you like the class—the wear-marks one?"

"It's OK. Or *was*, up till now. It counts for a social science."

"You should have taken Cecile's oil stains."

"She saw them first. It was really nice of her to offer, though."

Hayden snorted a laugh.

"What?" said Myra.

"Nothing. Except she wasn't being *nice.*"

"What do you mean?"

"She didn't wanna be ditched. She offered you her oil stains so we wouldn't go off and do something without her."

"Why do you say that?"

"Because it's true. She's the jealous type."

"She doesn't seem that way to me."

"Just you wait. See what happens when you get a boyfriend."

Myra didn't like this remark. They walked in silence for some time. At Rollins, they crossed over and walked by the new Student Center.

"Do you mind if we duck in here?" said Hayden. "I need to get a drink."

"Certainly," said Myra.

They entered the complex. It wasn't particularly busy, even for Saturday. The coffee bar was closed.

"Cal's is open." Hayden led the way to the indoor hamburger stand. There he ordered a fountain soda.

Myra hadn't intended to get anything, but when she saw the waffle fries, she suddenly became hungry. She ordered a small paper boat of the fries and a drink.

They took their orders to a tall, circular table and sat down on the tall chairs.

Myra had eaten only a few of her fries when she said to Hayden, "You wanna finish these?" She pushed the boat across to him.

"Oh—thanks!" he said. He began eating the fries. "First thing I've had all day!"

Myra had noticed that when he got his drink, he paid for it with cash rather than with his meal card. She wondered whether he wasn't on the low-budget Bronze Plan.

Hayden asked her, "So are your parents coming up for Family Weekend?"

"No. I told them not to bother."

"Where're you from?"

"Kansas City."

Hayden nodded. Another reason, he perceived, that he and Myra were not destined for each other. He was from Caruthersville, in the Bootheel. They might as well have lived in different countries.

"Your parents coming up?" Myra asked.

"No."

She didn't ask where he was from.

"What makes you think Cecile is the jealous type?" she said.

"Because she is."

"How long have you known her?"

"We met at orientation. She ditched her tour group and joined mine. She just came up to me and told me she liked my tour group better." Hayden frowned. "We were walking over to Bradley Hall. Now it's like we're best buddies. Only I'm always on call and if I don't want to do something when she wants me to, like give her a ride to Target, she gets snippy. We have to go to Target practically every other day."

Myra said, "If you don't want to do something with her, then *don't*, and she'll stop asking."

"Maybe."

"Just say *no*."

"You have a car?"

"Yes."

"That figures."

"What do you mean?"

"You'll be able to give her rides, too."

"You mean that's all she cares about?"

"No, it's not all she cares about. But it binds you to her."

"*Binds* me to her?" Myra laughed.

"She'll become dependent on you, and then, you know, you can't let her down. You'll feel sorry for her."

Myra tried to think if she felt sorry for Cecile. She didn't think she did.

"Is that how you feel?"

Hayden didn't answer this question.

"Just because she doesn't have a *car?* Most students don't have a car—do they?" Myra herself drove a green convertible Mazda Miata. It had been a high-school graduation present from her parents.

"It's not that she doesn't have a car," said Hayden. "It's that you feel *obligated* to her—to *help* her. And don't think she doesn't know it."

Myra saw that the waffle fries were gone. Hayden had eaten every last morsel.

"You're hungry!" she said. "You want a hamburger?"

"I'm OK."

"Let me get one for you!"

Hayden was surprised by the kind offer.

"It's the least I can do," Myra said. "Or we could split one. You wanna split a hamburger? I couldn't eat a whole one." She frowned. She was concerned for Hayden's welfare.

"No, I'm OK. You ready to go?"

They got up and left the Student Center and continued on to Blitzing. Neither of them spoke until they arrived outside the entrance to the glass-box structure. There was a sign stuck in the grass in front, hardly more substantial than a "For Sale" sign, identifying the building.

"Arthur Blitzing Hall," Hayden read from the sign. They were standing at the bottom of six elongated concrete steps that led up to the two glass entrance doors. There was a light on in the foyer, but otherwise the building appeared to be completely dark.

"So this place has a lot of wear marks?" said Myra.

"We can check out the men's room in the basement. There's some pretty crazy graffiti. One of the doors is off one of the stalls."

"I'm not going into the men's restroom!"

"I could take a picture—"

"No. That's gross."

"OK."

Hayden ascended the steps and tried the handle of one of the two doors; then he tried the handle of the other door. Myra stayed where she was.

"Uh-oh," he said. Now he was pulling on both door handles simultaneously. "The place is locked!"

"What!"

He turned around.

"The building must be closed on the weekend."

"Oh, crud!" Myra was disappointed.

Hayden came back down the steps.

"Sorry."

"It's not your fault."

"You wanna try someplace else?"

"Like where?"

"Atchison?"

"No—Cecile doesn't want us to. She'd have to let us in."

"Tell me about what you were looking for at the library."

"*Due*-date slips. Only they don't use them anymore. Not the pasted-in kind."

"Cecile said something about marked-up books."

"There was one book I found that was an autobiography—it had notes written in the margins. I thought they would be good wear marks, but Cecile said that you couldn't interpret anything about who wrote them." Myra was trying to remember. "Like the guy was a Republican or something."

"They're still wear marks, aren't they?"

"But what do you say about them? They're supposed to reveal something."

"Do you have to say what they reveal about who *wrote* them? Can't you say what they reveal about the *book?*"

"Oh!" Myra thought it over. "You mean, like the book was good enough that it caused readers to write comments in the margins?"

"Or that it was *bad* enough. Or whatever. Just like on YouTube."

Myra thought some more.

"You could compare it with other books," she said, "ones that *don't* have comments. Why do some books get written in but not others? I mean, you could make a hypothesis."

"You could."

"Like textbooks! People are always writing in textbooks. And *highlighting.*"

"With those dumb-ass yellow markers."

"Yes!" Myra looked at Hayden. "*I've* never done it."

Hayden almost laughed.

Myra smiled.

"Shall we go back and check up on Cecile and her laundry?"

"Absolutely."

* * *

That evening Hayden joined Myra and Cecile at Shakespeare's. Myra had sent him a text message inviting him. The pizza was going to be her treat.

Hayden found the two girls seated at a table with their drinks.

"Hayden!" Cecile shouted.

"Hi." He sat down next to Myra.

"We ordered an extra-large Masterpiece pizza," Myra said, leaning towards him so he could hear. There was a din of voices in the popular establishment. "OK by you?"

"Yeah. Were you able to use the comments written in that book?"

Myra nodded.

"I went back to the library and looked through it. And other books, too, other autobiographies."

"Sounds reasonable."

"Tell him what you discovered," said Cecile, who was listening carefully. She was a loud talker.

"I discovered that no one else's autobiography had anywhere near as many comments. Most had none at all. So I had to figure out why, and that's when I came up with my interpretation."

"And what *is* your interpretation?" said Hayden.

"That if there are a lot of *comments* in the margins, then there are probably a lot of *opinions* in the book. In other words, the comments are a *wear mark* for that kind of book. I know it's not profound or anything, but—" Myra shrugged her shoulders.

"Who's the author of the book?" Hayden asked.

"Malcolm Muggeridge."

Hayden had never heard of him.

"He's British," Myra explained. "He's a journalist— or *was*. He had a lot of opinions."

Hayden got up from the table and went to get himself something to drink. When he returned, he had a glass of water in his hand. He sat back down.

Cecile raised her glass.

"To Malcolm—whatever-his-name-is!"

Myra raised her glass.

"To Malcolm!"

Hayden grunted. He raised his glass.

"And to *us!*" Cecile added. "We're the best!"

This produced an eye roll from Hayden, but he clinked his glass.

Myra leaned towards him and said into his ear, "Thank you, Hayden."

ROAD TRIP

Officially, Family Weekend began Friday evening and ended Sunday afternoon. Cecile's parents arrived on campus early Saturday morning. They lived in Mexico, Missouri, a town thirty miles northeast of Columbia, and they were delighted to be able to visit their daughter and participate in the day's scheduled activities. They had intended to come back Sunday as well, but late Sunday morning Cecile's mother called and told Cecile that her father didn't feel up to it. He was exhausted.

The change of plan left Cecile with nothing to do for the day. She texted Myra asking if she wanted to meet for lunch. Myra texted back that she couldn't meet for lunch because at that moment she was on her way to Johnson's Shut-Ins State Park, over 150 miles away in the St. Francois Mountains. She was with friends from Rivard, her residence hall, and they were traveling in three cars to go swimming in the rock pools. Cecile asked her if she was going to be back in time for dinner. Myra replied that she was not.

That afternoon, Cecile did some internet research. When she was finished, she texted Hayden. She waited for a reply, but no reply came. She proceeded to call him.

"Hello?" Hayden answered guardedly. He had seen the text message.

"Hey! How 'bout it? Road trip next weekend!"

"Why do you wanna go on a road trip?"

"For fun! We'll invite Myra. Just the three of us."

"Where?"

"I was looking at different places. It doesn't have to be *far*—"

"Where do you wanna go?"

"I was thinking of Arrow Rock. It's only about forty miles away."

"What's Arrow Rock?"

"It's this cool little town on the Missouri River. It's on the whatchamacallit trail. They have all these old houses and stuff. It'd be like stepping back in time!"

"And you want me to drive you there?"

"I want you to drive *us* there. You, me, and Myra. You'll like Arrow Rock. It's educational."

"What's there besides old houses?"

"There's an old tavern. And a visitor center."

"Anything else?"

"There's the Bus Museum."

"The *Bus* Museum?" Hayden didn't care for museums.

"It's just gonna be a fun trip. We'll walk around in the sun. Summer's practically over, and soon no one's gonna want to go anywhere."

"How long will it take?"

"*I* don't know—look, if you don't want to do it, just say so, and we can forget about the whole thing."

Cecile was getting snippy.

"No, we can do it," said Hayden.

"Good. I'll tell Myra. Hopefully, she won't have other plans. I think we should go next Saturday. There's no game next Saturday, is there?"

"It's an away game."

"Excellent! Listen, I need to get some stuff at Target. Can you take me tomorrow?"

"Sure."

"Hayden, you're a pal!"

When Cecile presented the road-trip idea to Myra, Myra wasn't quite sure what to make of it. She didn't know anything about Arrow Rock other than that there was a highway exit sign for it on I-70 between Kansas City and Columbia. The way Cecile described it, it didn't sound terribly promising. But since Cecile was so eager to make the trip, Myra said she would go. Her only worry was the amount of work she had to get done. She had to finish reading *Middlemarch* by the following Monday. If Saturday was going to be spent with Cecile and Hayden, then her reading schedule during the week would have to be strictly adhered to.

Unfortunately, there was a complication. One of Myra's residence-hall floormates, a junior named Gibby, had taken an interest in her. He was among those Myra had gone with to Johnson's Shut-Ins State Park in the St. Francois Mountains. He ought to have fallen into the category of Potentially Eligible. He was tall and good-looking and wasn't a freshman. The problem was that, as her floormate (even on the opposite end of the floor and separated by the elevators and the common area), he was too close for comfort. After they returned from Johnson's Shut-Ins, he got into the habit of dropping by her room to chat when she was trying to study. "Hey, Myra! Got a minute?" he would say. Then he would stay for half an hour. He also got into the habit of accosting her when she was on her way out of the building in the morning and barely functional. "Meet for coffee after Spanish?" he would say. He knew her schedule.

It wasn't all Gibby's fault. Myra should have been firmer with him. She should have taken her own advice to Hayden to "just say *no*." But Myra didn't take her own advice, and by Friday she had fallen behind her schedule. This made her angry with herself. Late Friday afternoon she decided she had better tell Cecile she couldn't go on the road trip after all. She would spend Saturday catching up on *Middlemarch*.

She hadn't yet informed Cecile of her decision when Gibby tracked her down in the glass-walled study lounge on the ground floor of Rivard just off of the reception desk. She was sitting alone, reading her book.

"Hey, Myra!" Gibby plopped himself into the chair next to hers.

"Hi, Gibby."

"I've got a feeding proposition for tomorrow. Interested?"

"A feeding proposition?"

"Dinner at the Gopher Hole! It's in town. There's also the option of going dancing afterwards." He named a local club.

"I don't think I can." Myra shook her head.

"No dancing—"

"No dinner either. Sorry."

"What is it—too much to do?"

"I have this book to finish. And a ton of other stuff."

"But you'll still need to get something to eat, won't you? We could make it just a quick bite someplace."

Myra was determined not to get any more involved with Gibby than she already had.

"To be honest, I'm spending tomorrow with friends, and I'm probably going to be getting dinner with them."

"Whatcha up to, Myra?"

The die was cast. She told Gibby she was going to Arrow Rock with Hayden and Cecile. She had to explain to him what she knew of the historic town, based on what Cecile had told her, including the existence of the Bus Museum.

"The Bus Museum!" Gibby chuckled. "Sounds fascinating. You can give me a full report."

"Yeah."

"You wanna go grab something to eat *now*—when you're finished reading?"

"I'm not really very hungry."

"All right. Another time. I think you're gonna like the Gopher Hole—"

"I dunno. I'm pretty busy these days. Getting busier and busier."

"Your work, huh."

"Yeah."

Gibby looked at her book and smiled.

"We'll talk later." He reached over and gave her shoulder a little pat and got up from his chair.

* * *

At eleven o'clock the next morning Myra, Cecile, and Hayden, along with Myra's roommate, Elena, set out in Hayden's subcompact for Arrow Rock. Myra had asked Cecile if she could invite Elena because Elena had expressed interest in the town. Cecile didn't really like the idea of another person coming along but couldn't think of any reason to object. Myra and Elena sat in the back seat of the car.

Sometime after they had gotten onto west I-70, Elena said, "We should sing!" They were traveling along the interstate highway at approximately seventy miles per hour. "We always sing when we drive." Elena was from Brazil. "I mean, in my *family*."

It was Myra who began the singing.

There *was* a farmer had a dog,
and Bingo was his name—O!

Cecile and Elena joined in for the refrain.

B-I-N-G-O!
B-I-N-G-O!
B-I-N-G-O!
and Bingo was his name—O!

Cecile, who was musical, modulated one semitone higher for the second verse, and Myra and Elena followed her lead.

There *was* a farmer had a dog,
and Bingo was his name—O!

Cecile began to harmonize.

[clap]-I-N-G-O!
[clap]-I-N-G-O!
[clap]-I-N-G-O!
and Bingo was his name—O!

Hayden, a non-singer, kept a tight grip on the steering wheel.

After six verses and four more modulations, the thing was done and there was an outburst of female laughter.

"Hayden, did we help you with your driving?" Myra asked.

"Yeah," said Hayden. "Thanks."

"I'm *so* excited about seeing Arrow Rock!" gushed Elena. "How much farther?"

"That was the Missouri River that we crossed back there," said Hayden. "We'll be coming up to Boonville next—"

"You're driving awful slow," said Cecile. "Everyone's passing us."

"No they aren't!"

"It's gonna take forever at this rate."

"OK." Hayden sped up by about five miles per hour.

"I think we better get something to eat in Boonville," Cecile turned her head to address Myra and Elena. "You guys OK with getting something to eat in Boonville?"

"Sure," said Myra.

"Sure," said Elena.

"You don't want to wait until Arrow Rock?" Hayden said to Cecile.

"That might be a little pricey."

At the second exit for Boonville there was a McDonald's. Hayden took the car through the drive-through and placed everyone's order. Five minutes later, they were back on the interstate, eating their food. When the exit for Arrow Rock came, they got off the interstate and proceeded in a northwesterly direction on an undivided state highway, one lane in each direction. The landscape now came closer and more pleasantly into view. There were no billboards, just cornfields, greenery, and the occasional farmhouse. The sun was shining, and puffy white clouds dotted the blue sky.

"Eleven more miles," said Hayden.

Myra, Elena, and Cecile were busy with their phone screens.

"Huh?" said Cecile without looking up.

"Eleven more miles till *Arrow Rock*."

"Uh-oh!" said Myra.

"What's wrong?" said Elena.

"It looks like Gibby might be joining us." Myra had been texting with him.

"Who's Gibby?" said Cecile.

"He's on our floor in Rivard. He's a friend, sort of."

"I think he wants to be your boyfriend," said Elena. She had noticed Gibby's attentiveness.

"What the—!" said Cecile. "Why is he joining us?"

"He says that since I wasn't going out with him to-night, he decided to drive home to Kansas City for the weekend, and it would be so easy to swing by Arrow Rock on the way and see what all the excitement was about. I told him I didn't know how long we were going to stay, but he's coming anyway."

"Where is he now?"

"He's just setting off. Sorry. I didn't know this was going to happen."

"Hayden, speed it up, will you? Maybe we can stay ahead of him." Cecile did not want Gibby joining them.

Hayden had been doing around fifty. He now sped up to almost seventy. Fortunately, there was hardly any road traffic in either direction. They passed only two ve-hicles. No one passed them.

Hayden was still doing close to seventy when a sign appeared in the distance on the left-hand side of the road. The sign was in the rustic style of the Missouri State Park system, with yellow lettering on a brown background. Hayden slowed the car down.

He read aloud from the sign: "Arrow Rock State Historic Site Visitor Center." An arrow below the lettering pointed to a turnoff on the right. "What do we do? Do we go to the Visitor Center?"

The turnoff for the town was still ahead of them.

"Better go straight into town," said Cecile.

Presently they passed a City Limit sign. According to the sign, Arrow Rock had a population of fifty-six.

"What about the historic marker?" said Hayden. They had just passed a sign reading, "Historic Marker ½ Mile."

"Just drive into town," said Cecile.

At the historic marker there was a junction with a store at the corner. Here Hayden made a right turn onto Main Street, and they entered the town proper. They passed a few white frame houses. As they got closer to the historic section, some brick buildings appeared and the houses became fancier, some with deep porches and white picket fences in front. Finally, they came to a row of one-story brick storefronts with a covered boardwalk running alongside. At the end of this row was a two-story structure, across the street from which was the stand-alone J. Huston Tavern. These buildings marked the end of the tiny business district.

"This is nice!" said Elena.

Hayden parked the car next to the tavern and they all got out. There wasn't anyone on the street but themselves.

"What'll we do first?" said Myra.

"Let's walk," said Cecile. "I wonder where all the people are."

"I wonder where the river is."

The was no sign of the Missouri River's proximity. Beyond the business district was open green space that ended in a thick bank of trees.

Cecile led them onto the covered boardwalk, and they began walking past the storefronts, moving up the street in the direction they had driven in from. Cecile set a brisk pace, so that no one had much of a chance to linger and look in any of the storefront windows. When the boardwalk came to an end at a cross street, Cecile said "Let's go this way and see what we find." They turned up the cross street, but at the first opportunity turned again. After two more turns, they were back at the car.

"We could go into the old tavern," said Myra. She was looking at the entrance to the J. Huston Tavern.

"I think that's basically a restaurant," said Cecile. "I mean, if you wanted to get something to *eat*—"

"What about the Bus Museum?" said Elena.

Cecile frowned.

"Do you really want to?"

"Don't you think we should?"

"Then we gotta ask where it is." Cecile pointed to one of the storefronts on the boardwalk. "Hayden, go in and ask. And *hurry*." She looked up the street to see if any car was approaching. There was none.

"Hello, hello!" said the proprietor as soon as Hayden entered the establishment. It appeared to be some kind of folk-art gift shop.

"Could you tell me where the Bus Museum is?" said Hayden. He was the only customer.

"Come again?" The proprietor was a bespectacled man with a trim gray beard and black eyebrows.

"The Bus Museum."

The man looked puzzled.

"There's no Bus Museum in Arrow Rock."

"There isn't?"

"No, sir!"

"Oh! We thought there was."

"Unless you mean the *Toy* Museum."

"Maybe that's what we were thinking of."

"But it's not in Arrow Rock." The man shook his head.

"Where is it?"

"It's more like a second-*hand* store than a museum. That's what I've heard. I've never seen it." The man smiled. Through the window he could see the three young women standing by Hayden's car. "Where you folks from?"

"Columbia."

"Going to college?"

"Yeah."

"That's a special time!"

"I guess it is."

"You have to enjoy it while you can. I went to Ann Arbor, if you can believe that. Back in the dinosaur era!"

"Ann Arbor—"

"The University of Michigan. You didn't see *The Big Chill*?"

"No—"

"It's a special time!"

"So do you know how we would get to the Bus Museum—"

"The *Toy* Museum. Like I said, I've never seen it, so I can't recommend it. Can't recommend against it either."

"Do you know how to get there?"

"Well, there's a sign for it. You can try following the sign."

"Where's the sign?"

"It's past the cemetery. You'll see a sign for a turn-off."

"The cemetery—"

"Get on TT across the highway, at the end of Main Street. Just go straight and keep driving."

"TT. OK, thanks."

"You're very welcome. You folks been to Arrow Rock before?"

"No."

"I hope you'll come again!"

"Thanks. We will."

Hayden left the shop.

"We need to get in the car," he said to Cecile.

They all got in the car, and Hayden executed a U-turn and headed back up Main Street.

"It's called the *Toy* Museum, not the *Bus* Museum, for Lord's sake!" he said.

"Oh!" said Cecile. "I thought it was called the Bus Museum. It's supposed to have this cool collection of buses. According to the website."

"They must be toy buses," said Elena.

"We're going to look at toys?" said Myra.

"Yeah," said Hayden. "I mean, if that's what everybody wants."

"Sure—why not?" said Myra.

"Why not?" said Elena.

They came to the end of Main Street and crossed the highway and got onto County Road TT. The village of Arrow Rock was now behind them.

"Where's the place located, exactly?" said Cecile.

"I don't know," said Hayden. "We follow the sign."

Elena said to Myra, "Are you going to tell Gibby where we're going?"

"*No.*" Myra powered off her phone.

They drove along the blacktop road past the cemetery and fields of mown grass and ripening corn. For a considerable distance there was no sign or advertisement for their destination. Then a small white wooden signpost appeared at the corner of a Y-intersection with an arm pointing right. Hayden slowed the car. He saw that the sign was inscribed "Toy Museum" and made the turn. They were now on a gravel road. Flanked by scrubby trees and dusty undergrowth, the road bent to the right in a large arc. When it straightened out, the natural vegetation left off and towering banks of corn rose. The corn came up so close to the road on both sides that the effect was claustrophobic. Hayden instinctively pressed his foot on the accelerator, the sooner to get the oppressive stalks behind them.

The straightaway ended at a blacktop road, where there was another signpost for the Toy Museum. Hayden turned in the direction indicated and began to bring the car back up to speed. The next signpost came up rather suddenly, so that he was obliged to hit the brake pedal hard. Once again, they were shunted onto a gravel road. This road led through fields of grass and was relatively pleasant to travel—except that the bends in the road seemed always to go to the left. Hayden wondered if they weren't moving in a giant circle. Then the road began to bend to the right, and Hayden felt better. Eventually they came to a signpost pointing to a narrow dirt road leading into some woods.

Hayden made the turn. As they bumped along the uneven lane, low-lying branches brushed against the windshield and the sides of the car. A cautionary white arrow appeared ahead of them announcing a bend to the right. Then another arrow appeared announcing a bend to the left. Then the woods came to an end.

And there it was. The small, two-story white frame house stood facing them across a graveled parking lot. There was a sagging roof over the front porch, and attached to this covering was a hand-lettered sign that proclaimed, "Toy Museum and Gifts." Behind the house was a plowed field.

Hayden parked, and they all got out. There was only one other car on the lot.

"I'm scared!" said Elena with a self-conscious smile.

Myra took her arm.

"We're going to have a fine old time!"

"Let's get this over with," said Hayden.

They proceeded up the walkway to the porch and climbed the steps.

Hayden was the first to see the sign next to the door.

"What the—!"

The sign read, "Admission $10.00."

"I'm not paying ten dollars!" said Hayden.

"I don't mind if we don't go in," said Elena. "I'm happy either way."

At this moment the door opened, creaking on its hinges.

"Hello and welcome to the Toy Museum!"

Before them stood a tall, bulky man with a bushy gray beard like a giant wire brush. The beard was nicotine-stained around the mouth.

"Hello," said Hayden.

The man, who was wearing black-rimmed glasses, stepped back and held the door open. Nobody moved.

"Admission is free of charge today!" This was a regular gambit. The man found that if he invited people in "free of charge" they were more likely to buy something.

The four adventurers filed in.

"There's a toy museum in Branson that claims to be the world's largest. But size isn't everything—ha ha!"

The room they entered was surprisingly spacious, taking up almost the whole first floor of the house. Several metal support posts had been installed where interior walls had once stood. The stairs leading up to the second floor were at the back.

"Please, step this way." The man ushered them to an oversized table in the center of the room. The table had been made by clamping two ping-pong tables together side by side, and on this an exhibit was set up. The exhibit took the form of a miniature town center with a grid pattern of streets and plain blocks of wood for the buildings. The featured items were the little die-cast cars, trucks, and buses that occupied the streets. There seemed to be hundreds of them.

"This is Car Town," the man said. "There's nothing quite like it. Not anywhere."

Hayden stood by the table and regarded the scene with a stony face. Almost all the toy vehicles were of the Matchbox and Hot Wheels type familiar to him from childhood.

Cecile was standing next to him. Myra and Elena took up positions alongside the table next to Cecile.

"It's a revolving exhibit," the man said. He picked up one of the little cars and put it in the breast pocket of his white, short-sleeved shirt. He then stepped over to a nearby shelf and selected a replacement car. He gave the car to Hayden. "Would you install this Ford Escort in Car Town?"

Hayden put the car down on one of the streets.

"You understand vehicle placement! The way you placed the car just right. Everything has to be part of the whole. Did you come far to get here?"

"From Columbia," Cecile answered.

"You came by Arrow Rock?"

"Yeah."

"Did you see Blackwater?"

"No—"

"You should see Blackwater." The man smiled. "I can give you directions."

Cecile looked at Hayden. Hayden was staring at Car Town.

"It's historic," said the man. "A nice little town. You can visit on the way back to Columbia. Meantime, please look around the Toy Museum."

"OK. Thanks," said Cecile.

"All the exhibits are in this room."

The man went over to a desk set up near the door and sat down on a swivel chair. From his position there, he was able to keep an eye on his visitors as well as the parking lot through one of the front windows.

Hayden turned from Car Town and looked around the room. Nearly all the wall space was taken up by bookcases of different sizes. On the shelves were displayed the same kinds of die-cast cars, trucks, and buses that were on display in Car Town. Nothing else.

Hayden made for the door. The man at the desk rose from his chair and intercepted him.

"There's an exhibit over here I think you'll like!" The man smiled as he took hold of Hayden's arm. "Please!" He conducted Hayden to a bookcase in the corner of the room nearest his desk. "This is the Christmas Shelf!"

The bookcase was stocked with cars in Christmas colors of red and green. Plastic holly leaves were stapled to the outside of the bookcase to enliven the scene.

"It's a personal favorite," said the man. "I like to think every day is Christmas. That's why the Christmas Shelf is on display all year round."

"Makes sense," said Hayden.

"I thought you'd appreciate it. Of course, it's not a religious representation. Everything is in very good taste."

Hayden nodded.

"Now, you just make yourself at home and enjoy the museum!"

The man returned to his desk.

Cecile joined Hayden at the Christmas Shelf.

"You OK?" she said.

"Sure."

"Cool museum!"

Hayden kept his eyes on the red and green cars.

Myra and Elena had begun their own tour of the shelves, passing slowly from one bookcase to the next. The man at the desk watched them.

"It's a nice day, isn't it?" he said.

Myra turned her head and smiled agreeably. She and Elena kept moving and eventually came to a bookcase on the far side of Car Town in the corner of the room diagonally opposite to where Hayden and Cecile were standing. The bookcase was stocked exclusively with buses.

"This must be the famous bus collection," said Myra quietly.

Elena picked up a red London Transport doubledecker. On the underside was a price tag. It was marked $25.00.

"Everything is priced," said the man at the desk. "Take your time."

"Are you thinking of buying something?" Myra asked Elena.

Elena was looking at the London bus. There was an advertisement for Typhoo Tea on the side.

"This makes me sad!"

"Why?" said Myra.

"Because it's tiny."

"What about that—whatever it was—Ford Escort?"

"Even that! Especially that!"

"Aw!"

"I'm going to buy this bus for my brother. He's going to be nine. Is that too old?"

Myra didn't have any brothers herself. She was an only child.

"I don't think so."

"Good! Because I love this."

Hayden and Cecile were still at the Christmas Shelf.

Hayden said under his breath, "How much longer we gonna stay?"

"What's your hurry?"

Hayden turned and looked across the room at Myra. She and Elena seemed happily occupied. He looked at the man at the desk, then returned his attention to the shelf.

"The guy's not gonna let us out of here unless we buy something."

"You sorry you came?" Cecile reached for the shelf and picked up a green sports car. The car was priced at $69.00. "Jeez!" Then, with her other hand, she picked up a red sports car. This car was priced at $99.00. "*Jeez!*"

"Everything is priced," said the man, looking at Cecile. He got up from his desk. A car had just driven into the parking lot. Cecile put the two sports cars back on the Christmas Shelf.

The man opened the creaky entrance door and stepped out onto the porch.

Presently he said, "Hello and welcome to the Toy Museum!"

"Hello," came the visitor's voice.

Myra recognized the voice at once as Gibby's.

"Come right in. Admission is free of charge today. We're always glad to welcome another patron." The man came back inside the house. "The toy museum in Branson claims to be the world's largest, but size isn't everything—ha ha!"

When Gibby came in, he spotted Myra immediately. He grinned.

"Hi, Gibby," said Myra.

"So this is the Toy Museum!" Gibby looked around and gave a little wave of his hand to Hayden and Cecile, whom he had never met.

"Now, over here," said the man through his bushy gray beard, "is Car Town. It's the centerpiece of our collection." He led Gibby to the exhibit. "There's nothing quite like it. Not anywhere."

Gibby took a look and said, "Neat! Excuse me a sec, will you?" He left the man at the table and went over to where Myra and Elena were standing at the bus shelf. "Hey, Elena!" To Myra he said, "You didn't stay long in Arrow Rock."

"Well," said Myra, "we were all pretty anxious to come *here*."

"I'm going to buy this bus!" Elena held up the red double-decker for Gibby to see.

Gibby smiled at it.

"I tried to call you," he said to Myra, "but it went straight to voice mail. It took me a while to find the directions to get to this place. I thought it was called the *Bus* Museum."

"That's what we thought it was called," said Myra. "But there's more to it than just buses." She made a limp gesture with her hand to indicate the entire room. "As you can see."

Gibby looked over at Hayden and Cecile.

"Will you introduce me to your friends?"

Myra summoned Hayden and Cecile, and the introductions were made.

"I'm glad I didn't miss you a *second* time," Gibby said to Myra. "I drove like the wind! Maybe you did, too."

Nobody responded to this.

"What next?" Gibby said.

"Blackwater?" said Myra.

"Blackwater! I've heard of it."

"The man said we could see it on the way back to Columbia. It's—" Myra looked at Cecile. "What did he call it?"

"Historic. That's all we know; what the man said."

"Yeah—historic. A nice little historic town. Like Arrow Rock."

"I'd love to see it!" said Gibby.

"I better pay for my bus." Elena took her bus to the man, who was sitting back at his desk.

"You don't mind if I tag along, do you?" Gibby said to Hayden.

"Me? No," said Hayden. "Are we *going* to Blackwater?"

"Why not?" said Gibby. "I can follow in my car. Any time you're ready."

"Don't you want to see the rest of the museum?" said Myra.

"I've seen enough."

"I'll get directions," said Hayden. He left to join Elena at the desk.

"Shall we?" said Gibby. He, Myra, and Cecile followed Hayden.

"It's been an honor," said the man when his visitors were ready to leave. Gibby had his hand on the door pull. "Please come again. We're open six days a week, Tuesday through Sunday, ten till six or by appointment. You can also find us on the World Wide Web." The man gave Hayden his business card. "The web address is on the card. I do most of my business on the web, you know."

"OK, thanks," said Hayden.

"Good-bye!"

When they were all outside, Gibby took Myra aside.

"Listen, you wanna come with me in my car? It must be kind of crowded with Elena and the rest." Gibby drove a high-riding red Jeep Wrangler SUV.

"No thanks," said Myra.

"You sure?"

"I'm sure."

Elena, Hayden, and Cecile were getting into Hayden's car.

"I can't believe the guy's gonna follow us!" muttered Cecile. "Doesn't he know when he's not wanted?"

Myra joined them.

"OK, let's go!" She took her seat in the back next to Elena.

"Is he really gonna follow us to Blackwater?" said Cecile.

"Yeah."

Myra wasn't any happier than Cecile that Gibby had attached himself to their party, but she wasn't going to let it spoil her afternoon. Hayden started the car and backed it out of the parking spot and drove into the woods. After he made the turn from the dirt road onto the gravel road, he brought the car up to speed. Myra unbuckled her seat belt and turned to look out the rear window.

"Is he behind us?" Elena asked her.

They were kicking up a certain amount of dust from the road surface.

"He's eating our dust!"

Cecile unbuckled her seat belt and turned to look. Hayden looked in the rearview mirror.

"Go faster!" said Cecile.

"What?" said Hayden.

"Go faster!"

Hayden obeyed the command. The amount of dust being kicked up increased considerably.

"I'm not gonna watch this." Myra faced forward and rebuckled her seat belt.

"Hayden!" said Elena. She was frightened.

Hayden eased his foot off the accelerator, slowing the car.

"Go *faster!*" said Cecile.

"No." Hayden was firm.

They rounded a bend, and a yellow sign appeared that read "SINGLE LANE BRIDGE 5 MPH." Hayden applied the brakes, and something went *pop!* He pulled over to the side of the road and brought the car to a complete stop.

"What are we stopping for?" said Cecile. The yellow sign ahead of them was attached to a kingpost truss bridge that spanned a creek bed. The bridge was clear and there was no vehicle waiting on the other side to cross.

Hayden got out of the car. He knew even before he looked that it was the driver's-side front tire.

"It's a blowout." He reached into the car and popped the trunk open. "Everyone's gonna have to get out."

Gibby pulled up behind in his Jeep. His tires were the rugged, knobby kind specially made for rough road surfaces. He got out of the vehicle and approached Hayden, who was bending into the trunk of his subcompact.

"What seems to be the trouble?" said Gibby.

The others were just getting out of the car.

"Blowout." Hayden extracted the spare tire, which was the "donut" kind, thinner and less substantial than a regular tire. On it was written, "Maximum Speed 50 MPH." Hayden put it down leaning against the bumper.

"That's a piece of bad luck!"

Hayden got out the jack and jack handle and the lug wrench and took them around to the driver's-side front tire. Cecile, Myra, and Elena were standing by and moved out of the way to watch.

The jack was a scissor jack that had to be placed directly under the jack-up point on the underside of the car. Unfortunately, the road was so rutted that Hayden couldn't get the jack to stand level.

"What you need is a stabilizing board," said Gibby. He went to his Jeep and brought back a length of 2 x 6 board. "Here. Work this into the gravel till it's level. Then put the jack on top of it."

"Oh—thanks." Hayden took the board.

"I never go anywhere without a piece of board in the car. Comes in handy when you're dealing with this kind of road surface or a soft shoulder."

Hayden got the board and the jack in place and began activating the jack.

"Don't jack it up yet," said Gibby.

"Why not?"

"You need to loosen the lug nuts first. If you try loosening them with the wheel off the ground, the wheel starts spinning round and round."

Following Gibby's instructions, Hayden abandoned the jack and took hold of the lug wrench and applied it to one of the nuts. It was a short-handled wrench, and, try as he might, Hayden couldn't get the nut to budge.

"The problem," said Gibby, "is your wrench. I'm guessing it came with the car? You really need a four-way cross wrench or an extended-handle wrench."

"Do *you* have one?"

"I do!" Once more, Gibby went to his Jeep. He returned with a four-way cross wrench. He removed Hayden's wrench from the nut and applied the cross wrench. It took but a firm twist with both his hands, and the nut was loosened. "See? You can get one of these at any good auto-parts store."

Gibby loosened the remaining nuts and then told Hayden to jack the car up. The tire was duly changed and the car lowered. Gibby tightened the nuts onto the spare.

"Well, thanks for your help," said Hayden when they were finished.

Myra felt obliged to say something.

"Yeah, thanks, Gibby. I guess we were lucky you came along."

"Thanks, Gibby," chimed in Elena.

Cecile said nothing.

Gibby smiled.

"No biggie." To Hayden he said, "You want to get that tire repaired as soon as possible. The donut is just for temporary use."

"OK," said Hayden.

"And don't go more than fifty miles an hour on it."

"I know."

Gibby addressed Myra: "Are we ready for Blackwater?"

Hayden said, "Maybe we better just go back to Columbia."

"We can make it a short visit, can't we?" said Gibby. "We'll be passing through there anyway, right?"

"Yeah."

"There'll be a place with visitor information. When we get there, we can decide what we want to do. Something to eat or drink wouldn't be out of order. Hopefully, they'll have espresso—right, Myra?" Gibby picked up his cross wrench and stabilizing board. "If we're ready—let's go!" He went back to his Jeep.

The blacktop highway leading into town went over the Blackwater River and through a railroad crossing and then turned into Main Street. On either side were the historic brick storefronts. A dark green vertical banner attached to a lamppost read, "Welcome—Founded 1887—Blackwater." The street was wide, and in a line down the center were a number of trees standing in octagonal planter boxes spaced at intervals. Between the planter boxes were diagonal parking spaces, almost all of them unoccupied. Hayden drove slowly. "Tell me where you want me to park," he said, eyeing the parking spaces. Gibby's Jeep was following close behind. Hayden received no reply to his request for parking instructions. His passengers were silent. Soon the commercial district was behind them and they were driving past houses. Then the houses left off and they were back among the cornfields.

"Well, that was Blackwater," Hayden said.

Gibby continued to follow them for the two and a half miles to I-70. There he turned onto the westbound on-ramp for Kansas City.

"Gibby's getting onto 70 West," said Hayden, who had been watching in the rearview mirror.

"He's going home for the weekend," said Myra.

"Good riddance!" said Cecile.

Hayden got onto 70 East. He had to keep the car's speed under fifty miles per hour on account of the donut, and as a warning to other vehicles he turned on the blinking hazard lights. All the way back to Columbia, cars, trucks, and buses roared past them. It was nerve-racking.

It was not quite three o'clock when they got back to campus. Myra and Elena thanked Cecile for putting the trip together and thanked Hayden for providing the transportation. "Some trip!" Cecile grumbled. Myra and Elena assured her that they had had a good time. But the trip had not gone the way Cecile had hoped. Myra said she was sorry about Gibby. She knew that he had come after them only because of her. But she was too anxious to get back to her work to feel any profound regret. After Hayden dropped her and Elena off at Rivard, the two roommates went to their room and Myra lay down for a short nap. When she got up, she took her copy of *Middlemarch* to Loesser Library and found a nice, secluded spot where no one would bother her.

Cecile sulked in her room. Later she sent Myra a text. But Myra had purposefully left her phone switched off and so was not disturbed. Hayden spent the rest of the afternoon playing video games on his laptop. He had his work to do but preferred to lose himself in mindless activity. That way he didn't have to think about his ineptitude.

Only Elena was positively happy. She had her red London Transport double-decker bus and was going to send it to her brother in Rio de Janeiro in time for his tenth birthday.

THE BOYFRIEND

It was after Homecoming, some weeks later, that Myra acquired a boyfriend. She had made up her mind that something had to be done about Gibby. He was still being attentive and seeking her out in her room when she was trying to do her work. There hadn't been any more invitations to have dinner at the Gopher Hole or to go dancing. But he was coming up with other ideas for things they might do together. Did she like playing board games? Attending campus lectures? Going hiking? "Not particularly." Would she be interested in joining a student organization or discussion group? "Sorry, I'm not a joiner." What about taking a weekend class on cheesemaking? "Definitely not!" It was thrust and parry, thrust and parry.

She found her man one Friday morning after Spanish class. His name was Ty. He was one of her classmates. He had come up to her with some pale green flyers in his hand.

"We're having a party." He gave Myra one of the flyers.

The piece of paper gave directions to the location of the off-campus house where Ty lived with his housemates Chuck, Dory, and Matt. Normally, Myra wouldn't have even considered such an invitation.

"You can bring someone," Ty said.

"What's it a party for?"

"It's just a party!" Ty looked like an athlete, which in fact he was. But he didn't look like a jock. Myra got the feeling he wasn't very aggressive where girls were concerned.

"It's not gonna be anything wild," he said. "Good food, music—"

"And beer!"

"Yeah!" Ty chuckled. "And beer! It's gonna be tonight at six P.M."

"Tonight?"

"Uh-huh. Just show up any time after six. And bring someone with you if you want. Chuck, Dory, and Matt are all good guys."

"The four of you live in the house together?"

"Yeah. We're like brothers."

"I'll think about it."

"Great!"

Myra went to the party alone. There weren't many people in attendance and only two or three females besides herself. Talking with Chuck, Dory, and Matt while Ty stood by with a big grin on his face, she learned that the four housemates were friends of long standing. They were all from Farmington, Missouri, and had gone to the same high school and had made a collective decision to attend the same college. Now they were juniors, and they all played intramural football. Only Chuck appeared to have a girlfriend. Her name was Simone, and she was from Farmington, too. Myra drank only one beer, and she left the party early. But she made sure to thank Ty for inviting her and suggested they meet the next day, which was a Saturday, and have coffee together. She and Ty exchanged phone numbers.

If Myra's actions were calculated, they weren't cynical. She liked Ty. She also liked his friends, who struck her as good-hearted if a little goofy. She took care, however, to establish herself as the driver of her new relationship so that it proceeded wholly on her terms. She would sometimes give Ty a kiss on the cheek when he did something nice, such as bring her a flower, but that was as far as she let her attentions go in that direction. She insisted on paying for herself whenever they got anything to eat off campus, and sometimes she paid for both of them (she received a generous "college allowance" from her father in the form of a Visa Platinum credit card). As for Ty, he was more than happy to take his cues from her. Just having Myra to call his girlfriend and spend time with was a big kick, and he was grateful. He was also awed. He had never met anyone like Myra before.

The effect Myra's new status had on Gibby was all that she could have hoped for. When she told him she couldn't accept his invitation to drive up to Clark County to attend the Mule Festival in Kahoka because she was going to the game that Saturday with her "boyfriend," he said, "Oh—I see." It was awkward sticking it to him that way, but it did the trick. "Your *boy*friend! OK." He smiled and bowed himself out of her room without further comment. Thenceforth, he would give her a friendly "Hey, Myra!" whenever he encountered her on their floor in Rivard or anywhere else, but he didn't seek her out. It was a great relief.

The effect on Cecile, however, wasn't so happy. When Myra told her she was seeing a guy she liked whose name was Ty, Cecile greeted the news with feigned pleasure. But she was unable to keep up the pretense. The next morning when Myra approached her after Geology class, Cecile suddenly had very little to say to her. This had never been the case before. Cecile also stopped texting. There were no more invitations to meet for lunch. When Myra asked her point blank if there was something wrong, Cecile said she was just very busy with schoolwork. "Busy, busy, busy!" she said with a straight face.

Obviously, something *was* wrong. Myra decided she had better ask Hayden. She sent him a text inviting him to meet her at a coffee shop on North Ninth Street. She was going to find out what the problem was.

"I told you what the problem was at the beginning," said Hayden. They were seated at a table with their cups of coffee and two orders of baklava. "Cecile is the jealous type."

"What did you mean, exactly—"

"I meant she doesn't like to share. Especially if the person she has to share you with is a boyfriend."

"Why?"

Hayden shrugged his shoulders.

"You might like the boyfriend—what's his name again?"

"Ty."

"You might like *Ty* more than you like *her*."

"Oh, for God's sake!"

"He's taking you away from her."

"It's not as though Ty and I are going to get married and go live in Farmington. He's just fun to hang out with. There's no reason why Cecile shouldn't be able to get along with him."

"Has she met him?"

"No."

"Then it's probably not gonna matter what he's like."

"If she can't accept even the *idea*—I'm sorry, but that's going too far. I can't cut off the entire world just to make her happy."

Hayden looked at Myra without saying anything.

She went on: "She doesn't seem to have any friends except for you and me. Elena tried being friends with her. You remember at Homecoming when we all went on that Country Corn Hayride? Cecile ignored her the entire time."

Hayden remembered. On the hayride, they were sitting on bales of straw and Elena asked Cecile a question about straw versus hay and why they weren't sitting on bales of hay. Cecile wouldn't even acknowledge that the question had been asked. She pretended to be preoccupied with the passing view.

"I think she must be very insecure," Myra observed. "She must be lonely, too. We should do something with her. Something special."

"Like what?"

"Like the road trip to Arrow Rock—only not a road trip."

"Now you're making *my* mistake."

"What?"

"Catering to her because you feel sorry for her."

"I'm not *catering* to her. She has to meet us halfway, just like any normal person." Myra thought of her new friend. "Ty's very normal. He's studying physical education."

Hayden nodded. He didn't want to hear any more about Ty.

"And business, too," she added.

"I'm taking a class in business," Hayden said. "It's probably going to be my major."

"You never told me that!"

"I thought about trying for engineering, but there was no way, really."

"Engineering's hard."

"I didn't have the math, for one thing."

"Could we use your car to drive someplace? I mean with Cecile."

"My car?"

"Mine only seats two, and there'll be you, me, Ty, and Cecile. We could go to a restaurant or something. She likes food."

"You think she's gonna like being with Ty?"

"If she met him and got to know him—"

"Maybe."

"I hope *you'll* like him."

Hayden managed to produce a half smile.

That evening, as the dining halls were beginning to fill up, Cecile made the short walk from Atchison to West. She wasn't carrying her laundry hamper. She had her backpack slung around her shoulder. Among the newly purchased items inside were a screw-top bottle of white wine and some plastic glasses. She had texted Hayden that she was coming over. She wanted to see him. He had texted back, "OK."

They went up to his room. Cecile set her backpack down on his cluttered-to-capacity desk, on top of an open three-ring notebook. She took out two plastic glasses and handed them to Hayden, then took out the bottle, unscrewed the top, and poured the wine. After she found a place for the bottle on the floor, she and Hayden stood and drank. Neither of them spoke or looked at the other. Hayden had an idea of what was coming, but it surprised him how quickly Cecile got down to business. Before she had taken more than three sips of her wine, she put her glass down and pulled off her top and removed her bra. The immediate effect on Hayden was to send him to the door to make sure it was locked. Not that Hayden's roommate, Connor, couldn't walk in at any time. He had a key. Cecile then began rummaging around in her backpack. Hayden stashed his own glass and went to his bed, the lower of the standard-issue bunkbed, and sat on the edge and waited.

Less than fifteen minutes later, Cecile was back in her room in Atchison. The deed was done. She got out her phone and spent the next half hour playing a game in which the object was to get three in a row of matching-colored candies.

* * *

The trip to a restaurant in Hayden's car never came off. Cecile had responded to Myra's text invitation with two words: "Too busy." This curt refusal caused Myra's blood to rise. But she had done her part. She now felt that any move to renew their friendship would have to come from Cecile. Hayden's relationship with Cecile had deteriorated as well. She no longer came over to West to do laundry, and there were no more trips to Target. Hayden had to wonder whether their encounter in his room didn't have something to do with it.

Hayden was having a bad semester. When he signed up for classes, he had done so with a view to becoming a business major. He was taking the exploratory course from the business school, Business Foundations, as well as three courses outside the business school that all business majors had to take: English Composition, College Algebra, and Introduction to Microeconomics. He was also taking Survey of American History to the Civil War as part of the general education requirement. In every one of these classes, he was sinking: assignments were not turned in on time or at all, and readings were left unread. He had lost his motivation. When Connor asked him why he spent so much time playing video games on his laptop, Hayden replied, "Because I got nothing better to do."

This wasn't quite accurate. He was also looking at college websites. He knew he was headed for disaster where he was and reasoned that a change of school just might save him. Almost any school would do—as long as it was away from Columbia. He wanted to enroll someplace soon so that when he broke the news to his parents that he was leaving school in Columbia he could present his departure as a transfer. But it wasn't going to be a transfer; it was going to be a withdrawal. There would be no credit earned from any of his classes, just a column of W's on his transcript.

Hayden submitted the necessary withdrawal forms just ahead of Thanksgiving break. The break was for the entire week, and many if not most of the students who were driving home left school the Friday before as soon as they got out of their last class of the day. Myra set off for Kansas City Friday afternoon after returning from a field trip to the Grindstone Nature Area, an extra-credit event for People, Habitat, and Nature. Cecile left school even earlier; not caring to participate in the field trip, she had her mother pick her up right after lunch.

Hayden was still on campus Saturday evening. He came by Rivard, Myra and Elena's residence hall. He had texted Elena that he wanted to see her. Elena was staying at school over the break.

She let Hayden in at the front entrance to the building.

"Hayden!"

"I wanted to ask you a favor," he said to her.

"Sure—anything!"

They walked past the man on duty at the reception desk and stood by the wall of keyed letterboxes that looked like the ones inside the post office.

"Would you give this to Myra when she gets back?"

Hayden handed Elena a sealed envelope. On it was written *To Myra from Hayden.*

Elena held it and looked at it.

"After the break, you mean?"

"Yeah."

She looked at Hayden.

"Won't you be here?"

"No."

"Has something happened—a family emergency?"

"Oh no. Everyone's fine. Nothing like that." Hayden looked in the direction of the man at the desk. There was no one else around. The glass-walled study lounge was deserted.

"Do you want to come up to the room?" Elena said. "I was about to make some tea."

"OK."

Elena led the way up the stairs to the second floor. Hayden had never been in the room before. Like many another roommate duo, Myra and Elena had converted the original bunkbed into two separate twin beds and placed them on adjacent sides of the room. They had also repositioned the two desk hutches and the two chests of drawers. In addition to being good movers of furniture, Myra and Elena appeared to be excellent housekeepers. The beds were neatly made, the desks were tidy, and the floor was clear of the kind of items that always seemed to find their way onto the floor in Hayden and Connor's room—loose clothes, towels, bottles, pizza boxes, etc. There was one object in the room, however, that struck a jarring note. Sitting on one of the beds was an enormous electric-pink, prick-eared stuffed rabbit. It looked like the grand prize from a shooting gallery at a carnival.

Hayden steered his eyes away from the rabbit-creature and stood facing Elena.

"I'm just changing schools," he said. "I'm going to Middlewater College next semester."

"Middlewater College?"

"There's a branch close to my home town. I'll be able to commute to classes."

"Oh!"

"Yeah. Movin' on up!"

"But you're going to finish your semester here, aren't you?"

"No."

"What about all your classes?"

"I'm withdrawing from them."

"Oh, no!"

"Yeah. I'll probably leave tomorrow. I don't know. Maybe tonight. Listen, Elena, I just want to say that I'm glad to have known you. You're one of the nice people around here."

Elena didn't respond to this. Her eyes began to shine.

Hayden gave her a wry smile.

"So take care of yourself. You won't forget to give Myra the letter, will you?"

The letter was still in her hand. She held it up for him to see.

"Thanks."

"Do you want a cup of tea?" she said.

"No. I think I better hit the road."

"We'll miss you."

"I'll miss you, too."

"Myra will be sorry you left without saying good-bye."

"That's what the letter's for."

"Without saying good-bye to her *face*."

"Yeah, well, it can't be helped."

"Do you really have to go?"

"I'm just in the wrong place. I'm not doing my work. I'm on track—I *was* on track—for failing all my classes. Don't tell Myra."

"Don't *tell* her?"

"I just need to be somewhere where I can concentrate."

"Away from Myra."

Hayden didn't contradict this statement.

"I feel bad for you," Elena said.

"It's OK."

"If it's any consolation, I like you better than *him*."

"Thanks." The comment was appreciated. Hayden looked at the giant, prick-eared rabbit sitting on the bed. "Is that Myra's?"

"Yeah. She hates it."

"Is it from him?"

"Yeah."

"What the heck—it's not even Easter!"

"I know. I wish it would go away!"

"Well—there's the dumpster at the Student Center." Elena giggled.

"It's tempting!"

"I could toss it in on my way back to West."

"Better not."

"How 'bout I dump it in the country? No one would ever know what happened to it."

"*I'd* know."

"OK." Hayden conceded the point. "I better be going."

"Good luck, Hayden!" Elena extended her hand to him, and he shook it.

Hayden had met Ty only once. Myra had invited him to join her, Ty, and Elena along with Chuck, Dory, Matt, and Chuck's girlfriend Simone at a "luau" held in the front yard of one of the fraternity houses where Ty and his housemates had friends. The front yard had been roped off on three sides by a cord held up by metal stakes, and hanging from the cord were vertical sheets of black plastic (possibly trash bags taped together). Inside this enclosure there was a boombox blaring raucous music and people were dancing. Some of the fraternity brothers were going shirtless. Ty had seemed nice enough—outgoing, sociable, a good laugher at other people's jokes. And, of course, he was athletic. He played intramural football and was studying physical education. But Hayden couldn't help feeling that, at bottom, he was just plain ordinary. That someone like Myra, who was the opposite of ordinary, could spend her time and bestow her affection on someone like Ty seemed to go against the natural order of things. He simply wasn't her match.

It was perhaps snobbish of Hayden to feel this way, but that was the type of person he was. He was also, it had to be admitted, the jealous type. At the luau, it had chagrined him to see Myra acting so free and easy with Ty, even when she was just getting him a can of beer. Then sometime during the festivities Ty took his shirt off and Myra put a lei around his neck! It was supposed to be a moment of high hilarity. Myra was smiling, but she wasn't laughing. Of course, this didn't mean she was *sleeping* with the guy. That was unthinkable. Hayden must not think about *that!* All in all, it wasn't an afternoon very well spent.

After leaving his letter with Elena, Hayden headed back towards West. It was getting on towards eight o'clock. He figured it wouldn't take him more than five or ten minutes to pack up his things—just dump everything into his backpack and suitcase without worrying about mixing it all up. Almost all the clothes were dirty anyway. He would leave his key card at the front desk and a note for his RA and then call his parents and tell them to expect him late but not to wait up for him. In the morning, he would tell them about his new plans for college.

He left no letter for Cecile.

* * *

Hayden's letter to Myra ran as follows:

Dear Myra,

I hope you had an enjoyable Thanksgiving. I'm writing this letter to you because I'm not coming back after the break but wanted to say good-bye. I'm going to be taking classes at Middlewater College. I'll be able to commute from Caruthersville (where I'm from) and it'll be a lot cheaper. To be honest, the class I was taking in business wasn't going very well, so that's another reason for me leaving.

It was a privilege to know you. I hope you will always think of me as your friend even if we never meet again which I don't expect we ever will. I wish you all possible success with your studies and in your future life wherever that may take you in the years to come.

Sincerely,

Hayden.

Myra read the letter with a frown. She was sitting on the edge of her bed next to the stuffed rabbit. Elena was standing, watching her.

Why, Myra wanted to know, had he seen fit to leave school this way, without any warning? It seemed underhanded. Why hadn't he given her the chance to say good-bye? She read the letter to Elena and asked her if Hayden had said anything to her. Elena replied that he had said he had been on track for failing all his classes.

Myra was shocked.

"He said he was just in the wrong place," Elena continued, "that he needed to be somewhere where he could concentrate. He wasn't doing his work."

Myra stared at the letter in her hand. It was written on a sheet of lined, three-ring-notebook paper in neatly inscribed print except for the signature, which was in cursive. It looked to have been carefully labored over.

"I didn't know it was that bad."

"He didn't want me to tell you."

"Why?"

"Because he likes you."

"Did he say that?"

"No. But you know he does."

Myra folded the paper and put it back in the envelope. She shook her head.

"He should have told me he was going to leave."

"I agree."

"He should have said good-bye to me in person!"

There were only five days left of instruction. In nine days final exams would begin. A conscientious student, Myra decided that the best thing to do as far as Hayden was concerned was to delay any action until after she had turned in all her work. Then the pressure would be off and she could call him up and they could have a nice talk. She sent him a brief text message saying that she had received his letter and had read it and would get in touch with him after she had taken her last final.

* * *

The final for People, Habitat, and Nature went quickly. It was a simple matter of writing a paragraph or two in answer to the question, "What have you learned from this course?" Both Myra and Cecile knew what was expected. They wrote that they had learned to be more observant and aware of the world around them, to see connections in all things, even the smallest things, and to be mindful of the balance of nature as it was affected by the activities of humankind. Myra wrote that the course had made her a better citizen. Cecile wrote that the course had been empowering.

Afterwards, they met in the hallway.

"Well, thank God *that's* over with!" said Cecile.

"Are you ready?"

"Yeah. That's it for me."

"Do we need to stop by Atchison for any reason?"

"No."

"OK, let's go!"

They walked to the remote student parking lot and got in Myra's car. They were leaving for Caruthersville. Two days before, after an exchange of texts with Cecile, Myra had sent Hayden a text informing him that they were coming. Her communication with Cecile was the first the two had had since their estrangement. It turned out that Cecile had not been aware that Hayden had left school. She told Myra she was "very not happy" that he had left without saying good-bye. She added, "We should do something." Myra texted back "Yes, we should!" and then proposed the drive down. It would be just a day trip, but they'd have enough time to hang out for a while and say good-bye properly. "I'm in!" was Cecile's reply. Hayden's reply to Myra was, "Well, OK." He gave Myra his home address.

On the way out of town, the two stopped at a gas station at Route 63 and Grindstone Parkway. After Myra filled the tank, she and Cecile went inside the station store to buy snacks. The woman at the register was wearing a Santa Claus hat. High up on the wall behind the counter was a display of Santa Claus hats for sale along with some "trapper hats," the kind of hats that have the enormous fur-lined (or, in the present instance, fake-fur-lined) ear flaps that can be worn up or down. The hats had the characteristic upturned fur-lined front brim.

"Do you think Hayden would like one of those hats?" said Myra.

Cecile squinted at the display.

"One of *which* hats?"

"Not the Santa Claus ones."

Cecile had no idea.

"Shall we all get one?" said Myra.

They selected three identical trapper hats with black cloth coverings, and Myra paid. Myra was sure Hayden would like his hat. When the frigid weather came, it would keep his head cozy and warm the way nothing else could.

The route they chose to get to Caruthersville led in a southeasterly direction through Jefferson City and Rolla and across the Ozarks through Salem, Round Spring, Eminence, and Van Buren. Not the quickest route, but prettier than sticking to the interstates and going via St. Louis. The route continued through Poplar Bluff into the alluvial plain, where suddenly there seemed to be no trees and only farmland. Seventy miles past Poplar Bluff, in the Bootheel, lay Caruthersville, on the Mississippi River.

They arrived in the late afternoon and met Hayden at his house, where he introduced them to his parents, who were most cordial. When Myra presented Hayden with his trapper hat, he declared, "Just what I needed!" He put it on in front of the mirror. Everyone was very pleased with the effect. Hayden tried all three ways of wearing the hat: with the ear flaps up and the connecting strap over the head; with the ear flaps down and the connecting strap under the chin; and with the ear flaps down and the connecting strap not engaged, so that the flaps hung freely. He suggested that Myra and Cecile might like to see something of the town he lived in, so the three of them excused themselves from Hayden's parents and left the house. Myra and Cecile's own trapper hats were in Myra's car, parked in the driveway. Myra now retrieved them, and she and Cecile put them on. They wore them the same way Hayden was wearing his, with the ear flaps down, hanging freely. Then they all got into Hayden's car, parked at the curb, and proceeded to cruise around Caruthersville. Cecile sat in the back. They went past the high school, the public library, the county courthouse, the post office, the entrance to the casino, and the boat ramp at the park by the waterfront. Myra had never seen the Mississippi before. They talked about Hayden's plans for study at Middlewater College. He said he was looking at Criminal Justice Technology and Fire Science as possible fields. Cecile said she was sure a degree in either of those would be very marketable. At a certain point Myra mentioned that she needed to drink some coffee before she and Cecile headed back to Columbia, so Hayden drove them to the McDonald's in nearby Hayti, where they stayed until it started to get dark.

Outside Hayden's house they took photographs with the flash on. Cecile used Hayden's phone as well as her own and Myra's to get shots of Hayden and Myra standing together by Myra's car. Cecile had Myra take her trapper hat off the better to capture her lovely hair. Hayden then got shots of Cecile and Myra together. Finally, Myra said it was time to go.

She put her trapper hat back on and came up to Hayden. She looked at him sidelong.

"You're not gonna neglect your studies, now, are you?"

"I won't neglect them," he said. "Thanks for coming, Myra."

"We'll keep in touch, OK?"

"Sure."

"You should come up for a game. Do you know what the schedule is for spring?"

"You mean for basketball?"

Myra frowned.

"I guess there won't be any more football."

"Not until fall."

"Come up anyway! We can all go out to the Grind-stone Nature Area."

"OK."

"It's beautiful!" She put her arms around him, and the two stood for a time in a hug-embrace. Then it was Cecile's turn.

"You're a pal!" Cecile said, squeezing Hayden tight. Standing on her toes, she whispered something into the fur of his left ear flap. His expression changed and a slight flush came into his face.

The two girls got into Myra's car, and Myra started the engine.

"Tell him we'll write him a Christmas card!" Myra said.

Instead of lowering her window to relay the message, Cecile shouted it at Hayden with the window closed. Hayden just grinned. Myra then backed the car out of the driveway and into the street. As she swung the car forward, she honked the horn in a burst of good-bye beeping and Cecile waved her hand. Hayden waved back, and then he was behind them.

They took a different route back to Columbia from the one they had taken coming down. This time they followed the recommendation of Google Maps and went via St. Louis. On the way up I-55 they stopped in Cape Girardeau to have dinner at a Chinese restaurant called Old China. They drank oolong tea and read their fortune cookies. Cecile said there were some Chinese restaurants in Columbia that they should try after they got back from Christmas break. Myra said absolutely. She would see if she couldn't leave her Miata at home and come back with her mother's Honda Accord, which seated five.

"That way there'll be room for more of us."

Cecile sipped her tea.

"That sounds like an excellent plan," she said.

Our Guest

Chapter 1

This story begins one afternoon in late May of 1956 when I was eleven and we still lived in our house on Leaf Avenue in Narberth.

I was bumping along through my last two weeks of sixth grade, and when I got home from school for the day, I went into the kitchen and was surprised to find my father sitting at the kitchen table. He normally didn't get back from his law office until close to six. He was talking to my brother, Arnie, who had just returned from his first year at college. Arnie was leaning against the kitchen counter with his arms folded.

"Hey, sport!" Arnie said to me. It was his third day home.

"Hi!" I said.

"How was school?" my father asked me.

"Good."

"What did you learn?"

"We learned about explorers."

"Which ones?"

"Magellan. Him and another guy."

"Magellan—" said Arnie. "What did he explore?"

"He was the first one to go around the world—his *boat* was. He got killed before he could get back. The other guy got killed, too. I forget his name. He got eaten by cannibals."

"*Cannibals!*"

"Henry," my father said, "would you go upstairs and ask your mother to come down? I want to see everyone in the living room."

"Everyone?"

"Everyone. No one's in trouble." He said to Arnie, "There's something I want to tell you all."

Arnie's alert face registered mild surprise.

"Oh—certainly!"

"I'll go get her," I said.

My mother was in her study, a small room on the second floor across the hallway from my bedroom. This was where she wrote her letters and rested in the afternoon. I knocked on the door.

"What is it?" came her voice. She didn't like to be disturbed.

"Dad says to come down," I said to the door.

The door opened, and she came into the hallway.

"I didn't know your father was home."

"He wants to see everyone in the living room."

I went ahead of her down the stairs. My father and Arnie were waiting by the living-room entrance.

"George, you're home early!"

"Please—" My father conducted her into the living room to the wingback chair he usually sat in himself.

"Has something happened?" my mother said, sitting down.

Arnie and I sat on the couch.

My father stood before us and smiled.

"I haven't said anything until now because until now there was nothing definite." He looked at each of us. "We're going to have an addition to the family!"

I looked at my mother. She was looking at my father. Were we going to get a dog?

"Henry," my father said to me, "can you tell me where Argentina is?"

"It's in South America."

"Exactly."

"Where Magellan went through—"

"Yes, it is—"

"To the South Pacific Ocean. Are we gonna get a dog?"

"No. Let me explain. There's a young lady from Argentina by the name of Anna Maria. She's fourteen years old, from a good family—a prosperous family in Buenos Aires." He addressed my mother: "You know Gunther Falkenstein. He's been corresponding with the lawyer, Señor Marasco, based in Montevideo. That's in Uruguay. Gunther says the immigration hurdles have been cleared and that Ännchen is ready to go."

My mother stiffened in her chair.

"What in heaven's name are you talking about?"

"Ännchen is coming to Philadelphia."

"*Who?*"

"Anna Maria! The girl from Buenos Aires. She'll be second-in-command to you around the house and prepared to help in any way."

"In *this* house?"

"Yes."

"Do you mean you have arranged this?"

"Gunther made the arrangements." Gunther Falken-stein was the president and owner of Falkenstein & Co., an import firm in Philadelphia my father did legal work for. "Consulting with me. Ännchen needed to go to a family; Gunther has no family."

"You didn't think somebody should have consulted with *me?*"

"Well, until now, there was nothing definite—"

"Oh, George!"

"I think you're going to like Ännchen. I think you're going to see how useful she is."

"How will she be useful?"

"She'll help with the housework."

"When I already get more than enough help from Mrs. Kedlin, who comes in two days a week?"

"But in the kitchen—"

"I don't *want* anyone in the kitchen!" Suddenly my mother was furious.

"She'll be a big sister to Henry!" My father pointed a finger at me. "This is a rare opportunity, Clara. We'll learn about Argentina and South America. We'll learn about the pampas and all the things they do down there. And *Änn-chen*" (he enunciated her name with care; it was pro-nounced "En-shen") "will learn the ways of a North American family living in a North American city. Of course, we'll all need to exercise a little patience. We don't know how well Ännchen speaks English. How's your Spanish, Arnie?"

Arnie didn't respond to this.

"Have you forgotten," my mother said, "that Arnie is leaving for his job in Trenton soon? And that Henry is going away to camp?"

My father took some moments to stroke his upper lip with his thumb and forefinger.

"The fact is," he said, "Ännchen needs our help."

"What do you mean?"

"She needs to get out of Argentina."

"Why on earth—?"

"There's trouble with the government. The family is originally from Germany."

"Then why doesn't she go to Germany?"

"It's not that simple."

"But why does she have to come to *us?*"

"Because Gunther asked. It'll count as a great favor to him if we can take her in."

My mother took a deep breath.

"And how long will the girl be staying?"

"Ännchen."

"How long will *Ännchen* be staying?"

"Indefinitely."

My mother's response to this was to rise from her seat and walk out of the room. My father watched her leave, but otherwise remained as he was. We heard her footsteps on the stairs and, finally, the sound of the door to her study closing.

"Well?" my father said, turning to Arnie and me.

Arnie was the member of the family to whom the job fell to calm the waters when they got choppy.

"I don't know, Dad," he said evenly. "It sounds like it'll be quite a change."

"Of course it will."

"I think you and Mother are going to have to talk about it."

"Hmph!"

Arnie looked at me.

"Why don't I take Henry out for a walk."

"All right." My father gave us a nod.

"Come on, sport!"

Arnie and I left the house by the front door. We walked along our quiet suburban street with the afternoon sun at our backs.

"I don't want a *big sister*," I said. I was keeping my eyes on the sidewalk.

This was the term my father had used. Ännchen was going to be a *big sister* to me once she was installed in our house. He also said something about her being *second-in-command* to my mother. I interpreted this to mean she was going to be allowed to boss me.

"We don't *need* anyone else," I said, thinking of Mrs. Kedlin, who came in two days a week.

Arnie tried to put a good face on it.

"It won't be so bad. She'll be nice, and you can learn Spanish." He chuckled. "She may not even come. You never know with Mother and Dad."

This was true. Just because my father was capable of acting on a matter that affected the entire family without consulting my mother didn't mean my mother was going to take it on the chin. She could punch back if she had to.

Arnie talked about college. He told me about his favorite class, a survey history course that had lasted the entire school year. The class was unusual in that different professors had been brought in for different historical periods.

"What did they do that for?" I said, uncomprehending.

"Well, each professor's a specialist. He's an expert on the period—say, the ancient Greeks and Romans. Then for the medieval period they bring in another professor, who's a specialist on *that* period, and so on."

He said the professors had all been very interesting men. Then he told me about his roommate at college, a fellow by the name of DeWitt who was from Greenwich, Connecticut, and played football. I was barely listening.

Arnie didn't engage me in any more conversation after that. He let me ponder. We walked around the neighborhood for what seemed like a long time before returning to the house. When we got inside, I went straight to my room to do my homework. Then it was time for supper.

Chapter 2

The day before Memorial Day (or Decoration Day, as my parents still called the May 30 holiday), my father informed us that Ännchen was due to arrive in Philadelphia in just three days, on June 1. He had gotten the word from Mr. Falkenstein that morning. My mother's response was, "Well, then, we had better get to work, hadn't we?"

My mother had decided that her study would be Ännchen's bedroom. The room already contained a bed and a chest of drawers with an attached mirror. There was also a drop-leaf secretary desk and one chair. My mother emptied the chest of drawers of its contents and directed Arnie and my father to take the secretary desk and the chair out of the room and bring in Arnie's old kid-sized table desk and chair that he had used when he was in elementary school. They also brought in a wardrobe cabinet from my parents' bedroom that my mother said would do very nicely for a young lady "if she's tall enough to reach the hangers!" Despite her exasperation with my father, my mother was determined to do right by our guest and went so far as to make new curtains for the window and procure a new bedspread for the bed. "Something a little *cheerier*," she said. "The girl will be so far from home!"

But then there came a delay. My father wasn't sure what the problem was. Mr. Falkenstein asked that we just stand by. The delay vexed my mother, but she said that at least we were ready for her. But I wasn't ready for her. I wanted her to stay away.

It was during this period that Arnie said good-bye to us. My father was going to drive him to Trenton where he was taking a summer job at the law firm of Finback & Voss. Mr. Finback was a friend of my father's from law school. It was also during this period that my school term ended. The day of Arnie's departure was the second day of my summer vacation.

Arnie took me into the living room for a few parting words. He was dressed in his best suit. My mother had already said good-bye to him and retired upstairs in a state of upset. My father was out by the car, parked on the street, waiting for the leave-taking to be over with.

"Everything's going to be fine now, Henry," Arnie said to me. "You just be nice to Mother. Will you do that?"

I nodded.

"Try to be helpful."

"Why do you have to go?" I had been asking variations on this question since the middle of the previous week.

"You know why. I'm going to work!"

"Why can't you work here?"

"Because Trenton is where the job is."

"Why?"

He gave me a pat on the shoulder. My father had told Arnie that he only wished he could have offered him a job at his own law office but that the extent of his practice didn't permit his taking anyone on. My father was a solo practitioner. When he needed assistance at the office, he called in Mrs. Skelly, a freelance stenographer who took dictation.

"I'll send you a postcard, OK? And I'll be back for a visit soon. Trenton isn't far."

"OK," I said without enthusiasm.

We shook hands. Then he put on the new gray fedora my mother had bought him and walked out the front door. I followed as far as the front steps. I stood and watched as he and my father got into the car and drove away.

Arnie had been with us barely two weeks. Now he was gone. That evening at supper, my father announced that Ännchen would be arriving in Philadelphia the day after the next by train from New York. I thought it was an awful cheat.

"I hope you agree," my father said, "that we all need to be there at the station to meet her." He was addressing my mother.

"Of course I agree," she said.

"Do I have to come?" The last thing I wanted to do was meet Ännchen at the station.

"I would like it, Henry," my father said.

My mother explained: "If the girl is going to be living under our roof, it is our duty to make her feel welcome. That goes for every member of this family."

According to the latest information my father had, Ännchen was fourteen years old and spoke at least some English. Her family had been living in Argentina since before the war, but the family was now under a cloud owing to political developments in the country. The popular and democratically elected president, General Perón, had been deposed the previous year by a military cabal, and supporters of the former leader were being persecuted. Ännchen's father was a hotel manager by profession, but he had been enough of a Perón enthusiast to get himself hauled in front of the state prosecutor and told he was the subject of a criminal investigation. This action may have been intended only as a warning to him to keep his nose clean. Whatever the case, the political situation in Argentina was so fraught and uncertain, with rumors of a counter-coup by Perón loyalists (Perón himself had fled the country), that there was no telling what might happen down the line. This was why, my father explained, Ännchen had to come to Philadelphia. She was a *refugee*. She would be traveling with a Mrs. Banes, a woman from New York who had been engaged by Falkenstein & Co. to accompany her on the last leg of her journey.

We were late meeting the train at Thirtieth Street. The tracks for the long-haul trains run under the station building, and by the time we descended the flight of stairs to the platform the train was already in. Passengers were getting out and turning in our direction. My mother and I stood back while my father positioned himself in front so that he could scrutinize the arrivals as they walked by. My father had never met Mrs. Banes, and he didn't know what Ännchen looked like either. He was simply waiting for a likely-looking pair of females to come along, at which point he would introduce himself. But no likely-looking pair came along. We moved down the platform to see if anyone was waiting there, but no one was. There were no more passengers coming out of the train. The luggage truck came by, and my father was obliged to step out of the way.

"Well, this is strange!" he said as he turned towards my mother and me. Then he caught sight of someone back up the platform. It was a young woman, by herself, walking purposefully in our direction.

My father waited for her to come into speaking range.

"Mrs. Banes?"

The young woman smiled.

"Mrs. Banes is in New York." She came up to my father with an outstretched arm and hand. "I'm Anna Maria."

My father's jaw didn't drop, but it might as well have. "You're—*Ännchen?*" He shook her hand.

"I am." She had an accent.

She was dressed in a dark blue jacket and skirt that looked almost black in the subterranean light. Her blouse was dark beige, and she wore a wide-brimmed hat set at an angle, like Ingrid Bergman's at the end of *Casablanca* (maybe not a coincidence, I now have to think). Underneath the hat, her hair was coiffed towards the back, emphasizing her pretty face. And it *was* a pretty face, with brown eyes so dark that the irises seemed like extensions of the pupils. She had lipstick on and maybe powder, too, and her eyebrows were shapely and well defined. She wore black gloves and in one hand clutched an elegant little purse. The one thing she didn't look like was a refugee.

"I'm Mr. Hutlinger—" My father turned to my mother. "And my wife, Mrs. Hutlinger—"

I could feel my mother staring at her.

"How do you do, Mrs. Hutlinger," said Ännchen.

My mother didn't immediately answer this greeting. She nudged me forward.

"This is our son Henry," she said. "Speak, Henry!"

"Happy to meet you," I mumbled.

"Happy to meet *you*," Ännchen replied. She extended her black-gloved hand to me. The way she was made up, she reminded me of one of the ladies behind the perfume counter at Wanamaker's department store, only a more youthful version.

"Shake hands, Henry!" instructed my mother.

I shook Ännchen's hand.

My father said he hoped she was well. Ännchen replied that she was. He asked if she had had a pleasant train journey. She said that the train journey had been very enjoyable, that the state of New Jersey was very interesting to see.

"It's not a long journey," my father observed. "I suppose you came through Trenton?"

"Yes," said Ännchen.

"After Trenton you would have crossed into Pennsylvania."

"Pennsylvania!"

"That's our state. Across the Delaware River."

"That is a big river."

"Yes, it is!"

My father asked about her luggage. She said she had a ticket for her suitcases and would need to claim the suitcases from the luggage room. We started to move along the platform toward the stairs. My mother kept me by her side and let Ännchen and my father walk ahead of us.

"Philadelphia is the capital city of Pennsylvania, no?" Ännchen remarked.

"It's not the *capital*," my father said, "but it's the largest city in the state."

"But it was the capital, once, of the entire country."

"Indeed, it was! For ten years, in the 1790s."

We were about to make the turn to go up the stairs. My mother could contain herself no longer.

"Excuse me, but I don't understand," she said. We all stopped moving. "We were told you were fourteen years old. And why is Mrs. Banes not here?"

Ännchen's reply was matter-of-fact: "She wouldn't come with me. She said she wasn't going to help me because I was older. She said I could take care of myself."

My mother looked at my father, then back at Ännchen.

"How old *are* you?"

"I'm eighteen."

"Eighteen!" my father exclaimed. "Well, there must have been some sort of mix-up about that. We're very happy you're here."

"I'm very happy to be here, Mr. Hutlinger."

"Something must have gotten lost in translation."

"Eighteen!" my mother said. "I would have guessed considerably older than that."

Was it the stylish clothes and made-up face? That was part of it. There was also her manner. She didn't appear to be the least bit shy or flustered. When she spoke, she did so with complete ease and assurance.

"Even so," my mother continued, "I don't think Mrs. Banes acted properly. She should have come. I'm glad you were able to find your way on your own."

"Thank you, Mrs. Hutlinger," Ännchen said.

We started moving again. My father led the way up the stairs. I was behind Ännchen, and as we climbed up, I was presented with a nearer view of her trimly fitted form. Her hips were close to my eye level, and I fixated on the slick texture of her skirt as she moved. My mother told me to watch where I was going.

Upstairs, my father led us through the cavernous waiting room to the luggage room, where Ännchen's suitcases were ready for pick-up. A porter loaded them onto a hand truck, and we made our way out of the building to the street. The change from indoors to outdoors was not pleasant. Cars and taxis were pulling up to the curb to load and unload passengers and luggage, and the air was thick with heat, humidity, and exhaust fumes. My father told us to stay with the porter at the curb while he went to get the car.

After he left us, my mother addressed Ännchen. She had to speak over the sound of the traffic: "You must be tired from your trip!"

"A little tired," said Ännchen.

"This heat is very tiring."

"Yes."

"We can all have a rest when we get home." My mother cast an eye on me. "All except Henry. He never seems to get tired."

"It is like this in New York." Ännchen said.

"I suppose it must be warm everywhere. What time did you get in to New York?"

"It was six days ago."

"Six days ago!" Another shock for my mother. "But we thought you were just off the boat!"

"I came by airplane."

"But where did you live?"

"With my friend Jeanne." She pronounced the name the French way, *zhahn*.

"Your friend *John?*"

"*Jeanne*. She is a girl. She lives in Brooklyn. I met her coming from Miami."

"Miami!"

"Miami was the port of entry. It was a long journey from Montevideo."

"That's in Argentina."

"In Uruguay, across the Rio de la Plata. Montevideo is the capital city."

"But what did you do in New York for six days? Why didn't you come to Philadelphia?"

"I was expecting a cable from my father."

"A cable?"

"A bank cable. I have a bank account. Jeanne was very helpful to me to set it up."

"In New York."

"Yes."

Perhaps feeling she had asked enough questions, my mother turned her attention to the approaching traffic. She kept her gaze fixed in that direction until my father arrived with the car.

The porter stowed the suitcases in the trunk, and my father gave him some money. My mother said that Änn-chen would sit with her. "Henry, you sit in the front with your father." My father opened the passenger door for me. My mother let Ännchen and herself in at the back. Then my father got into the driver's seat, and we got under way.

Chapter 3

I was the first one into the house, ahead of even my father who unlocked the front door. I went straight to the kitchen and let myself out the back door into the back yard. Then I set out along the back property lines through the weeds and stink plants and hopped one or two low fences, eventually reaching the cross street at the end of the block. There was a stink plant that was growing by the telephone pole, and I stopped to make a whip. To make a whip you snap off one of the long stalks of the stink plant and pinch it just below where the leaves start. Then, holding on tightly to the base with your other hand, you slide your pinched fingers up the length of the stalk in a single, continuous motion. You end up with a little bouquet of leaves in that hand, and a gleaming fresh whip in the other. Both the leaves and the whip have a bad smell. Having made the whip, I started whipping things: the telephone pole, the stink plant, some grass, the sidewalk. But I soon became self-conscious: an eleven-year-old boy should not be engaged in such childish activity. I threw the whip away and walked along the sidewalk to the corner of the street.

From there I could see the car parked in front of our house. The coast seemed to be clear—Ännchen and her suitcases had been taken inside. I sniffed my hand: it had the bad stink-plant smell. I proceeded as far as the beginning of our property and ducked in at the side of the house where there was a water faucet. I rinsed off my hands and shook them out. Then I reentered the back yard.

Ännchen was there, waiting for me. She was no longer wearing her hat and gloves, and I saw for the first time all her dark brown hair, so neatly combed and pinned. Without her hat on, she didn't look as tall as she had at the train station. She wasn't much taller than I was, maybe five foot three. She stood in the center of our patchy back-yard lawn, motionless as a statue.

"Are we going to be friends?" She was smiling.

I averted my eyes and made a kind of half-approach to her, veering off before getting too close. When I halted, I focused my attention on a patch of discolored lawn.

"I've been thinking about my family," she said. "Do you want to know what I've been thinking about them?"

My eyes were on the grass.

"What—" I said.

"That my mother cried when I left but I didn't."

I didn't know what to make of this piece of information.

"I should be with them," she said without conviction. "With my mother and father. But I wanted to come to Philadelphia."

"Whuddja wanna come to Philadelphia for?"

"Because it is in this country. I'm going to be in motion pictures!"

This wasn't something my father had told us about. I looked at Ännchen with new interest.

"Which ones are you going to be in?"

"I don't know yet. First, I must go to Hollywood."

She smiled again. I tried to imagine her face up on a movie screen. It wasn't easy, given the back-yard setting.

"Do you like the pictures?" she asked.

"They're all right." I liked war and gangster movies best.

"We can go see one together! Would you like that?"

"I always go with my brother." This wasn't meant as a rebuff. It was simply a statement of fact.

"But he is away—in Trenton." My mother had told Ännchen about Arnie's summer job when we were in the car.

"That's where the job is," I said.

"The train made a stop in Trenton. I should have got off the train to go see him."

"You don't even know where he lives!"

"I'm only fooling." She brought a hand up to her mouth to cover a yawn. "Goodness! I'm weary!"

I began attending to the grass again.

"Your father took my suitcases up the stairs," she said. "I talked to your mother. Then I came out here to look for you."

I was concentrating on the sod in front of my right foot. With the tip of my shoe, I gave it a little kick.

"But I didn't see where he took them."

I looked at her.

"Where he took what?"

"My suitcases."

"He took them to your *room*. Across the hall from my room, on the second floor."

"I didn't see the room."

"You want me to show it to you?"

"Would you?"

"Follow me." I turned and started towards the back-door steps. Ännchen followed.

In the kitchen, I paused and said, "This is the kitchen." In the dining room I said, "This is the dining room." There was no sign of my parents.

In the dining room, Ännchen stopped to look at our old Queen Anne–style china cabinet standing up against the wall on its curved legs.

"That's the china cabinet," I said.

Ännchen peered through the glass-paned doors.

"So beautiful!"

She was admiring the never-used "Viennese Portrait Plates." These were eight plates propped up on two of the shelves for display. They had been given to my grandmother by my grandfather on one of their long-ago wedding anniversaries. But my grandmother would never have them out. She kept them hidden away in a box be-cause she thought they were indecent. Each plate depict-ed, in color, a different beautiful young woman elegantly coiffed and attired but with shoulders bared or cleavage showing.

"May I open?" Ännchen said, putting her hands on the knobs of the cabinet doors.

"Sure."

She opened the doors and looked at the plates more closely.

"Such beautiful faces! Where did you get them?"

"From my grandmother."

I ran to the front hall. From the drawer of the front-hall table I got a flashlight and brought it into the dining room.

"Look at this." I took one of the plates down from its shelf and pressed the flashlight onto the underside of it. Then I switched the flashlight on. A disc of light appeared at about where the girl's cleavage was. "The light comes right through." I moved the flashlight around to emphasize the effect. "That means it's porcelain."

"I didn't know that!"

"My dad's a collector."

"A collector!"

"I'll show you."

I put the plate back and returned the flashlight to its drawer. Ännchen closed the cabinet doors.

"Come into the living room," I said.

If my father was a collector, he wasn't a systematic one. He liked the Portrait Plates well enough, but he himself wasn't devoted to any particular theme, pattern, or style and had no interest in acquiring large sets. The way he collected was to pick up odd, individual pieces that struck his fancy—they could be plates, bowls, cups, jars, tiles, statuettes, thimbles, knife handles. The only requirement was that the pieces be interesting (to him) and be made of porcelain.

Ännchen followed me into the living room, and I indicated the mantelpiece over the fireplace with an outstretched arm as though to say "Behold!" The mantelpiece was crowded with porcelain bric-a-brac. Ännchen went up to take a closer look.

"So funny!" she exclaimed. She picked up a small figure. "What is it?"

The figure in her hand was a Billiken, a grinning imp-like creature with a large head and a large stomach sitting with its stubby little arms hanging down and its stubby little legs sticking straight out in front of it with the undersides of the feet and toes prominently displayed. My father referred to the figure as an idol.

"It's an idol," I said with an air of authority. "It's a good luck charm."

Ännchen laughed.

"I love it! He reminds me of you!"

I was taken aback. This was not a welcome comparison!

She returned the idol to the mantelpiece.

"But you're much handsomer," she added.

"You wanna go up to the room now?"

She flashed me a smile.

I led the way upstairs. In the upstairs hallway, we had to pass the door to my parents' bedroom. The door was closed, but we could hear voices within.

Ännchen stopped for a moment as though to listen.

"Your mother doesn't want me here," she said in a low tone.

This was perhaps true, but it disturbed me to hear Ännchen say it.

"Oh, they're just talking." My parents' actual words weren't audible.

"They were expecting a fourteen-year-old girl."

"Come on," I said, beckoning to Ännchen with my hand.

She followed me past the door to the bathroom, which I pointed out for her, and then we entered my mother's study, now Ännchen's bedroom. My father had put Ännchen's suitcases down next to the bed, which was located on the left-hand side of the room against the wall. It was made up with the new bedspread, which showed a jumbly pattern of zoo animals, red, green, and blue, on a white background.

"It is very nice." Ännchen was standing just inside the doorway. "You must have gone to a lot of trouble."

"No trouble at all."

At the window was Arnie's old kid-sized table desk and chair, and in the far right corner of the room, where my mother's drop-leaf secretary desk had recently stood, was the wardrobe. Ännchen stepped past me and went to the wardrobe and opened the doors and looked inside. She removed a wooden hanger and, turning around, inspected it by the light of the window. Apparently satisfied, she put the hanger back and closed the wardrobe doors. She then turned her attention to the chest of drawers with the attached mirror, which stood adjacent to the wardrobe directly across from the bed. My mother had laid a stack of fluffy white towels on top of it. Standing in front of the chest, Ännchen felt the surface of the uppermost towel with her hand. I thought she was going to open the drawers next, but she kept feeling the towel.

"Thank you, Henry," she said without looking at me.

"What are you thanking me for?"

"For being nice."

She kept her hand on the towel for a moment or two. Then she picked it up and retreated to the bed and sat down next to her suitcases. She clutched the towel in her lap.

"I'll rest now." She smiled at me as if to signal all was well.

"OK," I said. "Supper is at 6:30." I left her and closed the door.

Chapter 4

In many ways my parents were old-fashioned people. Our evening meal was supper, not dinner. Dinner was at midday or, on Sunday, in the midafternoon. My mother always prepared it from scratch, and my father always took a break from work to come home for it unless he was away visiting a client. There was no television or radio in the house, and the only record player we had was an old wind-up Victrola that had come from my mother's family along with about a dozen antique records. The Victrola was just a curiosity. If my mother wanted music, which wasn't often, she sat down at the out-of-tune upright piano in the living room and played something from the hymn book. My father liked to spend his evenings reading. His favorite author was Washington Irving (we had a set of his complete works). My parents never went to the movies.

It therefore came as something of a shock when the next day my father came home for dinner with a radio in hand. He came into the kitchen with it, where dinner was always served on weekdays. I was seated at the kitchen table, and Ännchen was standing with my mother, helping with the food.

"This is for your room," my father said to Ännchen. He set the radio down on the table. It was about the size of a large toaster. The housing was made of wood and there were four dials on the front.

Ännchen stopped what she was doing.

"For my room? A wireless?"

"Yes—a radio!"

"My goodness! Thank you!"

"Listening to the radio will be a good way for you to keep abreast of what's happening in this country—in addition to the newspaper." We took the *Philadelphia Inquirer*, which my father had shared with Ännchen that morning at breakfast. "And, of course, if you like music—"

"Can we get a TV set?" I said.

"Certainly not," my mother said. "And the word is *television* set. But the radio is fine, if you don't mind not playing it excessively loud, Ännchen."

"Of course, Mrs. Hutlinger. I shall be very quiet. Like a mouse."

My father grinned. It was obvious the radio had been his idea and that he hadn't consulted my mother. He moved it to the kitchen counter and sat down at the table.

"I think we're ready," my mother said. She looked at Ännchen. "Please sit."

When they were seated my mother closed her eyes and bowed her head for a moment of silent prayer. Ännchen bowed her head, too, just the way she had done at supper the evening before. That meal had gone reasonably well. Ännchen had done most of the talking then, describing her life in Argentina. She told us she had been born in Germany and had come to Argentina as a baby when her family emigrated in 1938. She spoke three languages: German, Spanish, and English. She said she learned German at home, Spanish at school, and English by going to films. Her father was the manager of a hotel in Buenos Aires, and she herself had worked at the hotel in various capacities, both behind the front desk and as head of *las mucamas*, or the hotel maids. She said she could tell us some very interesting tales about what went on in a large hotel! This remark caused my mother to raise an eyebrow. Ännchen said her mother worried that she was growing up too fast. She didn't approve of Ännchen's going to films, but Ännchen went anyway, often sneaking out in the evening. She said she had seen *To Have and Have Not* about eighteen times and had memorized almost all the dialogue and could sing the songs (including "Hong Kong Blues," which she sang for me one evening in her room using accompanying mime-like hand movements). The one thing Ännchen didn't talk about was her father's difficulties with the Argentinian authorities.

Now, at our midday dinner, my mother did most of the talking. She seemed to have gotten over Ännchen's apparent worldliness.

"George," she said to my father, "what do you think of asking one of Arnie's friends to take Ännchen to see some of our historic places in Philadelphia? They could visit Independence Hall. I think she might find the experience interesting."

"Would you like that?" my father asked Ännchen.

"It sounds wonderful!" Ännchen said.

"Which one of Arnie's friends did you have in mind?" my father asked my mother.

"Well, Keith Ganse has a car. Fran says Keith is a careful driver."

My father considered.

"What about Henry going along?"

"Me?" I said.

"Yes, you."

Keith Ganse had been Arnie's classmate at the Brinsley School, all the way from when Arnie started in the seventh grade through his graduation from the high school. Keith was a jerk. He was the kind of guy who, when your parents weren't present, made no secret of the fact that he didn't like kids, especially you. To be sure, Arnie never let him mistreat me when he came over to the house and I hung around asking a lot of pesky questions. But he would have gladly twisted my arm if he could have gotten away with it (while shoving me out the door). He didn't have any brothers or sisters and was the only person I knew whose parents were divorced. He lived with his mother and was supposedly attending Temple University.

"Would you like to come?" Ännchen asked me.

"I think it's a splendid idea," my mother said. She had caught my father's drift. Keith would be Ännchen's guide, and I would be her chaperone. A wise move, as it turned out.

"OK," I said.

My mother then gave Ännchen a short lecture on Independence Hall, the site where the Declaration of Independence was signed and the Constitution adopted. My father chipped in with some names and dates when my mother's power of recall failed her—he mentioned the painter Charles Willson Peale, for example, who ran a stuffed-bird and fossil museum on the premises from around 1802. Philadelphia's place in our country's history, renowned though it was, wasn't a subject my parents were used to talking about, even to me (I learned about history at school). My mother was obviously making an effort for Ännchen's sake. Ännchen, for her part, made the appropriate responses—"Yes?" "*Ach!*" "Really!" She responded the same way when the conversation touched on Bartram's Garden, a tree and plant preserve on the Schuylkill River that you could walk around in. Keith Ganse might be able to be of service there, too, my mother said. She would call Keith's mother.

"You're very good to me," Ännchen said. She looked at both my parents.

"You're part of the family," my mother said.

My mother was only doing what duty required. I don't think she had developed any affection for Ännchen at all. My father, on the other hand, seemed to like her, and I loved her.

And I mean *loved*. The night before, when I was supposed to be in bed, I went to her door to give her an unasked-for cup of water. She was about to go to bed herself—she answered my knock wearing a light-blue, ankle-length flannel nightgown, and her hair was unpinned and down around her shoulders. She had done all her unpacking, it looked like. The top of the chest of drawers showed a large collection of containers and bottles, plus there were combs and brushes laid out. On the table desk there was a stack of magazines, a book of some kind, a big sketch pad, a collection of pens and pencils, and a travel alarm clock. The thing that really caught my attention, however, was the framed photograph on the window sill. It was a black-and-white studio portrait of Ännchen looking very much like a movie star. Ännchen didn't invite me in—I was standing in the doorway—but she accepted my cup of water with a tender smile. She told me I was her *ally*. I wasn't sure what she meant by this (ally in what?), but I knew it was true. I knew there was nothing I wouldn't do for her.

"When can we go?" I said.

"I'll have to arrange it with Fran," my mother said. "I'll find out when Keith is available."

After dinner, my father carried the radio up to Ännchen's room with Ännchen and myself accompanying him. Ännchen made room for the device on top of the table desk, and my father put it down and plugged it in and switched it on. We had to wait some moments for it to warm up. When it had done so, my father adjusted the tuner and the volume and pronounced the reception to be excellent. He exhorted Ännchen to enjoy listening and departed for his law office, leaving the bedroom door open behind him.

Ännchen invited me to stay. She sat down on the bed close to the foot. Alone with her now, I was suddenly shy. I sat down on the bed close to the pillow. "Sit closer, Henry," she said. I scooched over towards her part way; she then scooched over towards me to close the gap completely. The radio was set to a station that was playing songs from the swing bands, and a female vocalist was singing. The combination of hearing this music and sitting so close to Ännchen was exhilarating. She was tapping her foot to the beat.

My father had left the volume at a low level, presumably in accordance with my mother's request not to play the radio excessively loud. Ännchen, however, soon got up and closed the bedroom door and went to the radio and turned the volume up. Smiling at me, she took her place back on the bed and resumed tapping her foot. Then, at the beginning of the next song—I think it was "Perfidia"—she got up and turned the volume up *again*. This time she didn't sit back down on the bed but took both my hands in hers and pulled me up to a standing position. She led me around a more-or-less fixed spot on the floor. This was my first experience "dancing," and I kept my eyes on my feet the entire time. Neither of us said a word.

Meanwhile, my mother made the call to Keith's mother. Keith was eager to be of service. He would come by with his car the next day, which was a Saturday, to take Ännchen and me to Independence Hall.

Chapter 5

He was very polite and fake-friendly inside the house. It was 9:30 A.M. We were in the front hall—Keith, my parents, Ännchen, and I. My mother was about to go out marketing. After Keith was introduced to Ännchen, he stood and listened to my parents talk about historical sites in Philadelphia as if he, too, appreciated their special value as windows onto the past, especially for someone like Ännchen, who was new to our country. He agreed with my parents that seeing Independence Hall was very rewarding and said he felt honored that they had asked him to take Ännchen there for her first visit. He said hardly anything to Ännchen directly and of course ignored me completely. Ännchen was turned out very prettily for the occasion in a floral-patterned sleeveless dress and a summer hat. She had red lipstick on and was wearing white gloves and clutching another elegant little purse. Once again, the total effect was to make her look more grown up than she was—or than we thought she was. She could have passed for one of my mother's younger married friends (if my mother had had any such friends). Keith was dressed up, too, though not in a way I approved of. He was wearing a dark jacket and a dark shirt and a dark tie. He looked like a gangster, but with no hat. He promised to return Ännchen and me home safe and sound.

The three of us went out the front door. Keith's little two-door hardtop was parked at the curb. I think it was a Nash Metropolitan. It was red and white.

"You're gonna sit in the back," Keith said to me, "and not be a pest, OK?" He tried to make this command sound friendly, but I wasn't fooled.

I got in the car. The back wasn't very roomy. There was a pile of loose clothes on the seat—Keith's unlaundered shirts, it looked like—and on top lay a tennis racket in its press. Keith held the door while Ännchen got in the front.

"What a funny little auto!" she said.

Keith got in and we took off. He was a brisk driver, to say the least. When he made the turn onto Lancaster Avenue, the car swerved so hard that I bumped my head.

"Hey!" I cried. The tennis racket had fallen to the floor.

"*Verdammt!*" Ännchen cursed. "Can't you drive more slowly?"

"Sorry." Keith turned his head to look at her. "So, you like to play the horses?"

"I like *horses.*" She was keeping her eyes on the road.

"We should go to the Garden."

"What garden do you mean?"

"Garden State Park. It's across the river."

"The Delaware River?"

"That's right."

"That's in *New Jersey,*" I said from the back seat.

"It's a racetrack. There're eight races a day. I'd be happy to take you."

"We're supposed to go to Independence Hall!" I objected.

"Will you pipe down? They run during the week. Not today. It's a great track. One of the best."

"It sounds exciting," Ännchen said. "But I only want to think about what we do today."

"You wanna cigarette? I got some Luckies."

"No, thank you. Are you old enough to smoke?"

He laughed.

"I've been smoking since I was thirteen!"

"What does your mother say about that?"

"She doesn't say anything."

"No?"

"I make my own decisions. She understands that." Keith had to hit the brake pedal hard when the car in front of us slowed down. "Goddam hillbillies!" he barked.

"Are we gonna get something to eat?" I said.

"We can get something to eat after we see the Hall," Ännchen said. "You'll have time for something to eat, Keith, won't you? Mr. Hutlinger gave me money."

"Mr. Hutlinger is buying?" he said.

"Yes."

"Then I have time. I know a place where we can go."

Keith pressed his foot on the accelerator.

We made it to Independence Hall without getting killed. The building had recently been taken over by the Park Service, and there was a Park Service ranger there to welcome us and be our guide. We joined a group of about six people waiting to take the tour. Ordinarily there would have been nothing for me to do but be bored stiff while the ranger lectured on and on about the different rooms and the furniture and colonial times and the Liberty Bell with its crack (in those days the bell was still housed on the premises). I had been to Independence Hall before. But with Ännchen, I was perfectly happy to hear the ranger out. He could have lectured in Swahili, and I would have been perfectly happy.

I kept close to her side. Keith didn't seem to be enjoying himself. Twice he told me to get out of people's way. The second time he attempted to shunt me away from Ännchen, but I wouldn't let him. Ännchen, meanwhile, was taking an interest in the tour.

Having covered the period of the Revolution and the Founding as well as the period during which Charles Willson Peale ran his stuffed-bird and fossil museum, the ranger spoke of Lincoln.

"'Half a million sorrow-stricken people were upon the streets to do honor to all that was left of the man they respected, revered, and loved with an affection never before bestowed upon any other, save the Father of his Country.'" The ranger was quoting from a news story from the April 24, 1865 edition of the *Philadelphia Inquirer*. The body of Abraham Lincoln was being conveyed through the streets of Philadelphia to Independence Hall, where it would lie in state for two days. "'The wet cheeks of the strong man, the tearful eyes of the maiden and the matron told more than it is possible for language to express.'" The ranger said over a hundred thousand mourners came to the building to pay their respects. "Philadelphia was the third stop on the great funerary procession."

"Where was the next stop?" asked Ännchen.

"The next stop was New York City. Then Albany, then Buffalo, then Cleveland, I believe—"

Our group was standing around the ranger in a semicircle. Among our number was an older middle-aged man and his wife.

The man said, *"Carrying a corpse to where it shall rest in the grave—"*

"Yes, sir."

"Night and day journeys a coffin."

The man's jaw was set. His wife took hold of his arm.

"It is sad," Ännchen said to the ranger.

"Yes, ma'am."

"Where did they *bury* him?" I wondered aloud.

Keith gave the back of my shoulder a shove. Apparently, he didn't think my utterance was appropriate.

"Ow!"

"Springfield, Illinois, young man," the ranger said.

"*O powerful western fallen star! O shades of night—O moody, tearful night—*"

The man's wife patted him on the arm with her free hand, and the recitation ended.

The ranger gave only a brief sketch of the history of Independence Hall in the twentieth century. The culminating event was the establishment of Independence National Historical Park by an act of Congress in 1948. The Park, which was still in the process of development, encompassed Independence Hall and other nearby historic buildings, and the ranger invited us to visit them all.

"Unless there are any more questions," he wound up, "this concludes our tour. It's been a pleasure meeting you all. Thank you for visiting Independence National Historical Park!"

When we got out of the building, Keith said to me, "Listen, you fruit, you do what I tell you when we're in there and behave yourself!"

"You're not my father."

"You couldn't *pay* me to be your father."

"You're not even old enough to smoke!"

Ännchen intervened: "It is time to get something to eat, no?"

I would have stuck my tongue out at Keith, but Ännchen gave me a warning look.

Keith took us to a place in West Philadelphia. It was an inexpensive restaurant that specialized in lunches. Since this was a Saturday, there were one or two families with small children seated.

"I didn't know this was a kid's place," Keith said as we sat down at a table. He and I sat on opposite sides with Ännchen sitting between us on my left.

"It is very nice," Ännchen declared.

The waitress came over with some menus. She was a busty, older middle-aged woman who wore a hairnet.

"And how are you fine folks today?" she said.

"We are well, thank you," said Ännchen, taking her menu.

The waitress listed the lunch specials, which were written on a blackboard in plain sight.

"Can I get you something to drink?" she said.

"Nothing for me," said Ännchen.

"I'll take a cup of plain black coffee," said Keith.

"Cream?"

"No."

The waitress turned her eyes to me.

"And for your boy?" Possibly she was nearsighted and wasn't wearing her glasses. I, of course, was mortified to hear myself referred to in this way, but not as mortified as Keith was. He shifted in his seat and made a throat-clearing noise.

Ännchen said to me, "*Liebling*, something to drink for you?"

"Yes, Mother," I said, suddenly playing the part. "Could I have some lemonade?"

"One glass of lemonade for the young man," the waitress said.

"Is that all right, Father?" I said to Keith. It was worth it just to see him squirm.

"I'm not your *father*. Get whatever you want. I don't care."

"Thank you, Father."

The waitress left with our drink orders.

Keith leaned across the table towards me.

"You really are a fruitcake! Now you've gotten that old bag thinking I'm related to you!"

Ännchen said, "Let's look at the menus."

When the waitress came back with my lemonade and Keith's cup of plain black coffee, we placed our food orders: Keith first, then Ännchen, then me. We all ordered the same thing, a grilled cheese sandwich. The waitress chuckled and said our family reminded her of the Three Bears. "Papa Bear, Mama Bear, and Baby Bear!" After she was gone, Keith drank his coffee in silence and smoked a cigarette. Ännchen entertained me with some toothpicks that she took from a container in the center of the table. She showed me the trick of removing the cherry from the goblet by moving just two toothpicks.

The arrival of the food seemed to improve Keith's mood.

"OK!" he said.

"Here we are!" said the waitress, distributing the sandwiches.

Keith bit into his and began chewing.

"*Bon appétit!*" The waitress left us.

"So, tell me," Keith said to Ännchen as he chewed, "what was it like during World War Two? In Argentina, I mean."

"Argentina was a neutral country for most of the war."

"What happened when it wasn't neutral?"

"We joined the Allies."

"But you're German, aren't you?"

"I was born in Germany. We left before the war— when I was still a baby."

"But while the war was going on, what did you do?"

"My father was manager of a hotel in Buenos Aires. He still is. During the war, I stayed at home. Later, I went to school. My mother helped my father."

"How come you left Germany?"

"So that my father could take the job in Buenos Aires. He spoke Spanish—his grandfather came from Spain. For him it was a very desirable step."

"Why?"

"The Hotel Immermann is first class. Important people stayed there. Except for the British. They had their own hotel."

"Did Americans stay there?"

"Yes, certainly. Even during the war."

We ate our food, and for a while nobody spoke.

When my sandwich was almost gone, Ännchen asked me, "Is it good?"

"Uh-huh."

"Henry, you should chew your food thirty-two times!"

"What about Keith?" His sandwich was almost gone, too.

Keith ignored my remark.

"You remember V-E Day?" he said to Ännchen.

"Of course. The day the war ended."

"In *Europe*. I remember V-E Day, all right, and V-J Day, too. You know, they say Hitler is still alive and living in Argentina."

"Not at my father's hotel. I would have found out!"

"But there are other Germans there. Everyone knows that. Maybe you met some of them."

"There are a great number of Germans living in Argentina. Most of them came to the country before the war. They are long established. There are German-language newspapers. I myself attended a German-language school."

"I meant *Nazis*."

Ännchen didn't bat an eye.

"It is true, you heard stories. Men who were former SS and had changed their names. But I never met them. Or if I did, I was unaware. You were not encouraged to ask."

"I guess that might be dangerous."

"Bad for business, my father said."

"The hotel business?"

"Everything."

Keith nodded.

"You like Philadelphia?"

"Very much."

"What are you gonna do next—I mean, what are your plans?"

"To be of help to Henry's family."

"How long you gonna stay?"

"I don't know. I hope to find out more when I meet Mr. Falkenstein."

"Who's he?"

"A business associate of Mr. Hutlinger's. He helped to bring me to this country. I meet him Monday."

"I hope you can stay long enough to go to the Garden. We can do other things, too." Keith looked at me. "Without the squirt."

I had to wonder whether Keith had ever been to the Garden himself. I thought for sure you had to be a grown-up to go to a racetrack, or at least to place bets, and that meant being twenty-one. Keith was Arnie's age, which was nineteen. On the other hand, he was undeniably a slick dresser. He'd probably been passing for older for years. He certainly fooled our waitress.

When we were finished, the waitress came with the bill and told us it had been a pleasure serving us. We got up from the table and went to the cashier. Ännchen paid and then made the mistake of asking Keith how much we should leave for a tip. She had the change from the cashier in her gloved hand. Without saying anything, Keith took her hand and opened her fingers and extracted a nickel. He then headed back to the table. A nickel would have been a very small amount to leave for a tip. Even I knew that. Ännchen knew it, too. She hesitated for maybe two seconds and then headed back to the table herself. There she plunked down more money. Keith said something to her, but whatever it was she ignored.

Across the street from the restaurant there was a neighborhood movie theater, and Keith suggested we go in and watch the matinee. Ännchen asked me if I wanted to, and I said sure. We weren't expected home until supper, so we had plenty of time. The theater was showing a double feature, and the movies were running continuously all day. We walked in during the main feature, which was a western. Ännchen had paid for our tickets, but Keith selected our seats—in the back row and to the right of the central aisle. I entered the row first, then Ännchen, then Keith, and we sat down. The movie soon came to an end, and when the lights came up Keith admitted that he had already seen it. There was a short wait before the next showing of the first feature, during which time two young members of the theater staff came in to sweep up. Keith asked Ännchen if she or I wanted any popcorn or candy from the lobby. That I was included in this offer astounded me. Ännchen said some popcorn would be nice. Keith got up from his seat, and when he was gone Ännchen gave my hand a discreet squeeze. She had taken her gloves off.

When Keith returned, he was carrying a bag of popcorn of the smallest size. He gave the bag to Ännchen, who passed it to me. Then the lights went down. There was a cartoon—I think it was a Tom and Jerry—and then the first feature began, a movie called *Vice Squad*. It had Edward G. Robinson in it and looked to be pretty good. About twenty minutes into the story, however, I noticed Keith's arm "resting" on the back of Ännchen's seat. In reality, his hand was on its way to her far shoulder—the one next to me. Ännchen, when she became aware of this stealth migration towards her bare flesh (her sleeveless dress only partly covered her shoulders), turned her head to look for the approaching hand. The expression on her face was strangely calm, and I wondered whether she wasn't going to let him complete the maneuver.

There was no doubt in my mind, however, that putting his hand on her shoulder was something he had no right to do. Before he could get there, I put my own hand on the coveted spot. Ännchen looked at me. Keith was looking at the movie, or pretending to, and didn't see what was coming. When his hand descended onto mine, it was as though it had come into contact with a high-voltage electric current. Reflexively, he snatched his whole arm away.

I won't tell you what he said to me, but it was enough for Ännchen.

"I think it is time to go." She stood up. I stood up, too. Keith remained seated. Ännchen told me to climb over the seat in front of me so I could get out.

"All right, all right," Keith said. He rose from his seat and moved to the aisle. I was as incensed at his behavior as Ännchen was—maybe more so. But I was sorry we were leaving. I wanted to see the rest of *Vice Squad*.

Outside the theater, Ännchen said that she and I would wait by the entrance while Keith went to get the car.

"Tell me now," she said to him, "that you are prepared to take us home immediately."

Keith gave her a puzzled look as though he couldn't imagine why she should say such a thing.

"Sure, I'm prepared to take you home immediately. Whatever you want." He went to get the car.

After we were under way, Keith once again brought up the idea of Ännchen accompanying him to Garden State Park racetrack. Ännchen said she would not be going with him, and that was the end of that. We rode the rest of the way home in silence.

Chapter 6

Ännchen let us in to the house with her key. When we were inside with the door closed, she stepped to the side window and looked out. She wanted to make sure Keith was gone. He had in fact driven away immediately, just as soon as we got out of the car.

Ännchen took her gloves and hat off and put them on top of the front-hall radiator cover.

"Are Mr. and Mrs. Hutlinger at home?"

They weren't in the dining room or living room.

"Henry, you were a true ally today."

"Keith's a fink."

"He has very bad manners. But we still had a good time, no?"

"Uh-huh."

She frowned.

"He was very rude to you."

"I didn't mind."

"After what he said to you in the theater, it was impossible to stay for the rest of the film. Do you understand that?"

"Yes."

"Do you?"

I didn't really, but I nodded.

She came up to me and took hold of my two hands in hers and held them for a moment. Then she put her arms around me.

I remember she had a nice smell: a bodily one but with traces of bath powder or perfume or whatever it was she kept in those containers and bottles on the chest of drawers in her room.

When she was finished hugging me, she said, "You don't have to tell your parents what happened in the theater if you don't want to."

"OK." I didn't think she was referring to anything more than Keith's behavior towards *me*.

"They will be curious to learn of our adventures." She smiled. "We had a good time, no?" she said once more.

"Yes."

"I'll go upstairs now and rest."

She didn't come down until it was time to get supper ready. My father and I were waiting for her in the kitchen with my mother. I had already told both my parents separately that Ännchen and I had had a good time, but not much else. They wanted to hear what she had to say.

She said that Independence Hall had been of the greatest interest to her. So much history in one building! She recounted some of the information from the ranger's lecture, including the description of the conveyance of Lincoln's body through the streets of Philadelphia. She said she would never forget her visit. This report very much pleased my parents. My mother congratulated herself on the idea of asking Keith's mother to enlist Keith as driver and guide.

My father gave Ännchen a quizzical look.

"And how was Keith?"

"He did everything I asked him to. But perhaps he's done enough for now."

"Done enough?" said my mother.

"For the time being."

"Did he behave himself?" inquired my father.

"He tried to *cuddle* with her," I said.

"Tried to cuddle?"

"At the *movie*—"

"You were my defender!" Ännchen said to me.

"I made him stop."

"Yes, you did—before anything started." She said to my parents: "I'm afraid Keith did not behave well the entire time. We went to see a movie—"

"It was called *Vice Squad*—"

"He was very rude to Henry, and we had to leave the theater and come home."

"I'm sorry!" my mother said.

"But we still enjoyed ourselves, no, Henry?"

"Uh-huh."

"I will speak to Fran about this," my mother said.

"Clara," my father said, "we don't want to put Ännchen in the center of a brouhaha."

"What brouhaha?"

"Well, Fran may not see things the way you think she will."

"What do you mean?"

"I mean after she hears Keith's version of—whatever happened. I don't want to say the boy is incapable of telling the truth, but she's going to believe whatever he tells her. You know that."

"George!"

My mother looked at Ännchen.

"I think it was enough that I insisted Keith take us home," Ännchen said. "I would not complain to his mother."

"If that's your wish," my mother said. "I certainly don't want to put you in the center of a brouhaha."

"Henry," my father said to me, "why don't we leave these ladies to their work!"

"Let me just say to Ännchen," my mother said, "that Mr. Hutlinger and I are very sorry if Keith's conduct was ungentlemanly."

"Yes, we are," my father put in.

"I'm sorry I ever *thought* of calling Fran!"

"It is quite all right, Mrs. Hutlinger," said Ännchen.

My father and I left them to the preparation of supper.

"Henry," my father said. We had come out of the back hallway into the front hall. We were out of earshot of the kitchen. "This afternoon, when you were in the movie theater—"

"Uh-huh."

"Were you able to watch most of the movie? A good portion of it, at least?"

"We saw to where the guy picked out the wrong man in the line-up. He picked out the policeman instead of the pickpocket—"

"Did Ännchen watch it, too, then—I mean, up to the time you had to leave?"

"Huh? Yeah."

He shook his head.

"All right. Go run along."

It was an odd exchange. Looking back on it, I can only conclude that my father was trying to find out whether Ännchen hadn't in fact allowed Keith to take liberties with her before I intervened. The idea was ludicrous, of course. But people will think the most improbable things when it comes to sex.

Chapter 7

The next day was Sunday, which brought up a problem about church. Though my mother was a believer and was always concerned about being a good Christian (by her lights), she wasn't an avid churchgoer. Most of the time she didn't go, and that meant none of us went. But every so often, maybe once or twice a year, she felt that the family needed to reacquaint itself with the ritual of worship, and we all had to start going. We had been in the middle of one of our going-to-church periods when Ännchen came to us.

The problem was that no one had thought to ask Ännchen about her church affiliation. Ännchen, it turned out, was Catholic. Our church was Lutheran. Ännchen assured my mother that she would be happy to go to our church, but my mother was afraid that if she did, she might be committing some sort of heretical act. She therefore offered to have my father drive Ännchen to the local Catholic church. But Ännchen said she didn't want to inconvenience us and make us late for our own church. Besides, she hadn't attended Mass in a very long time. My mother decided that if Ännchen wasn't going to go to her church, then we weren't going to go to ours either.

I think everyone, including my mother, was highly satisfied with this solution. We spent the morning doing *quiet* things (my mother's suggestion). Ännchen sat on the couch in the living room and looked through movie magazines, ones that she had brought with her from Argentina. They were in Spanish but had lots of pictures. My father retired to his study, and my mother read from a book. I wanted to sit with Ännchen and look at her movie magazines, but my mother told me to do something else. So I lolled around the house semi-bored and restless. This was my usual condition at home on Sundays. The rule was that I had to stay indoors until after dinner (served excruciatingly late on Sundays), at which time I was free to leave the house and seek out neighborhood friends.

But this Sunday I had no interest in seeking out neighborhood friends. I had to stay within hailing distance of Ännchen in case she needed me for anything. If it seems like I was overly attentive, I had a reason: in two weeks I was scheduled to be shipped off to Camp Mon-Su-Ming-Nee in the Poconos. It was galling. I had attended the camp the summer before and had quite liked it (I found out I was bad at canoeing, archery, and identifying flora and fauna but good at roasting marshmallows and hot dogs on a stick and playing capture the flag). But going away now meant leaving Ännchen for three whole weeks. Short of performing some act of self-mutilation, I could think of no way of getting out of it. When Ännchen asked me if I was excited about camp, I said, "I *hate* camp!" She and I spent the latter part of Sunday afternoon playing a card game she taught me called *Quartett*. The game used special cards that she had brought with her from Argentina. Instead of numerals and suits, the cards had pictures of marine animals on them. You played to get sets of four of the same kind of animal: *der*

Hai, for example, which was the shark. The game was practically the same as Go Fish.

Monday was the day appointed for Ännchen's meeting with Mr. Falkenstein. The purpose of the meeting, I was told, was to discuss her future. The idea of Ännchen's future naturally made me anxious, for it had to include the possibility of her leaving our house to go live somewhere else. My father was to accompany her to the meeting, which was scheduled for 10:00 A.M. in Mr. Falkenstein's office in Center City.

The day started off with some bad news. At breakfast, my father handed Ännchen the morning paper as she sat down at the table. He said, "I think you better see this." There was a story on page one with the headline "40 Rebel Leaders Executed As Argentina Quells Revolt." Ännchen read the story while my father drank his coffee and I drank my orange juice. Nobody spoke until Ännchen was finished reading. My mother, who was at the stove, said she was sure no one in Ännchen's family had been affected by the revolt. Ännchen's only response was to say, "It is in God's hands." She didn't appear to be overly concerned. My father said they would know more when they talked to Gunther.

When it was time for my father and Ännchen to leave, I asked if I could come, too. I was genuinely worried about the revolt. I was told I had to stay home. My father said he didn't know how long the meeting with Mr. Falkenstein would last or whether he and Ännchen would be back in time for dinner. As it turned out, they weren't back in time. My mother and I had dinner with Mrs. Kedlin, who had come in for one of her twice-a-week work days. My job on these days (when I wasn't in school) was to push the carpet-sweeper over the rugs in the living room and the dining room and empty the wastebaskets. That morning I performed the job without any fuss.

Ännchen never told me what transpired at the meeting. I found out eventually, but not until almost two years later, when Arnie told me what my father had told him (so my information comes at third hand). Mr. Falkenstein started off by giving Ännchen an account of his business, which was the importation of animal and plant fibers used in the manufacture of textiles. The fibers Mr. Falkenstein specialized in were wool, mohair, sisal, and jute. He explained that most of his wool came from Argentina and that it was through his company's lawyer in Buenos Aires, Señor Agustin, that he first learned of Ännchen's father's difficulties. Señor Agustin had been approached by Mr. Falkenstein's chief buyer, Señor Heinzelmann, who was an acquaintance of Ännchen's father and was trying to help him obtain competent legal advice. After learning the facts in the case, Señor Agustin informed Mr. Falkenstein of the situation and asked for instructions. Mr. Falkenstein urged Señor Agustin to do what he could, whereupon the lawyer in Montevideo, Señor Marasco, was retained. Mr. Falkenstein said he understood that Señor Marasco had attended to Ännchen personally, and Ännchen confirmed this. She said that he met her when she arrived in Montevideo and put her on the airplane when she left for Miami. Mr. Falkenstein said Señor Marasco's services had been the key to getting Ännchen to the United States. It was he, Señor Marasco, who suggested that Mr. Falkenstein become Ännchen's sponsor.

Mr. Falkenstein then asked Ännchen how much she knew about the trouble her father was in. Ännchen said she knew only that her father was facing possible prosecution by the Argentinian state. Neither her father nor her mother would tell her why. She asked Mr. Falkenstein if he knew, and he said he did.

He said that for a period of about fourteen months during the war, her father had been an operative for the *Abwehr*, or German Military Intelligence. The work consisted of reporting on guests at his hotel and occasionally accepting and delivering messages. The work ceased in the fall of 1943 when the man who was his contact, a German national like himself, mysteriously disappeared. The intelligence service was in fact about to undergo radical restructuring on orders from Hitler that would ultimately lead to its demise. Its demise was perfectly all right with Ännchen's father—he had been an unwilling recruit in the first place. But now the threat of prosecution hung over his head based on his wartime activities. The ruling junta in Argentina, which had come to power by deposing General Perón, had accused him of spying for the enemy, even though Argentina had not been at war with Germany at the time (Argentina declared war only in March of 1945).

Mr. Falkenstein was sure that the real reason Ännchen's father was being threatened was that after the war was over, he had been obliged to *resume* spying on his guests, only this time on behalf of the Perón faction. In other words, he had gotten involved in domestic politics, which was a much more dangerous game than spying for the Third Reich. And now here was the news that a revolt had taken place, instigated by Perón loyalists, and that it had been brutally crushed. Mr. Falkenstein showed Ännchen the headline from the *Philadelphia Inquirer*.

Ännchen told him she had already read the report. Mr. Falkenstein said he didn't want to speculate as to what the repercussions might be. He said he was just glad he had been able to help Ännchen get out of the country.

Ännchen shook her head and thanked him. She said she would always be grateful. She was sorry, though, if there had been any misunderstanding. She said the reason she left Argentina was not to secure her safety but to find her "true path." She wanted a certain kind of career for herself, and to have any hope of getting it she had to come to the United States.

Mr. Falkenstein must have been interested to hear this. He asked her if she didn't think she had been in any danger of arrest in Argentina along with her parents. Her reply was, "There is always danger from something." She said she hoped Mr. Falkenstein didn't regret what he had done for her.

My father spoke up and said he thought Ännchen's next step should be to enroll in some sort of school, such as a business college (that is, a secretarial school). Attending a school would be valuable in and of itself and would give Ännchen a recognizable connection to the community that would count in her favor when the time came to renew her visa or apply for permanent-resident status. Mr. Falkenstein thought this was a good idea and said he was sure there were more than a few good business colleges in Philadelphia that would be suitable. Ännchen said she would prefer a school in Los Angeles. Mr. Falkenstein asked her to explain. She said she wanted to be close to the motion-picture industry, that she had hopes of auditioning as an actress at a studio and was also interested in the possibility of finding employment as a "costumer" or costume assistant. She knew what made clothes look good on women and had already worked for a modeling agency in Buenos Aires, both as a model and a dresser.

When my father told Arnie about this meeting, he said he had to give Ännchen credit for determination. She knew what she wanted and was taking the steps to get it.

She would, of course, have presented her case in her usual calm and assured delivery. But there was also the sound of her voice. It had a slight lilt to it, even in the way she pronounced "ally" as "ell-eye." It was strangely arresting: it made you want to do whatever you could for her. But *perhaps* I'm projecting. Mr. Falkenstein said he understood her wishes and would look into the matter.

Chapter 8

The next day we received our first letter from Arnie. My father brought the unopened envelope into the kitchen at dinnertime.

"Finally!" my mother said, taking the envelope from him. The letter was to all of us, including Ännchen. The envelope was addressed in Arnie's neat handwriting to Mr. and Mrs. George Hutlinger, Henry, and Anna Maria. When we were all seated at the table, my mother bowed her head and then unsealed the letter.

"What's the news?" my father said. "Good, I hope."

It had been a week since Arnie left us to start his summer job at the law firm of Finback & Voss in Trenton.

My mother read aloud from the letter:

Dear family,

I'm sorry for not writing sooner. I am well and Mr. Finback seems to be happy with the work I'm doing, which keeps me busy. After work on Wednesday, which is when I started, I had to take a box full of papers to the Millers' that I had to go through. The Millers are the people who have the house I'm rooming in. Dad met them when we drove up. They're very nice. I had to take a box home Thursday, too, and I'm working on two more boxes over the weekend. We're not really supposed to take work out of the office, but there's so much and I don't want to fall behind. I don't know when I'll be able to get away for a visit home—

My mother put the letter down. "Oh, dear!"

"I don't like the sound of that," my father said.

"I was counting on a visit before Henry goes to camp!"

"What I'm wondering is, is the boy up to the job they've given him?"

My mother shushed him.

"If he can't visit us, then we'll visit him. We'll go to Trenton." She began to read the rest of the letter to herself.

"It doesn't sound like he'll have much time for us," my father said.

"I'll make a telephone call to Mr. Finback's office and speak with him. He'll tell me when and where we can meet him."

"Can I talk to him?" I asked.

"No, Henry. You'll see him soon enough. I will make the call."

"It'll be long distance, Clara," my father said.

"I know that." My mother continued reading the letter to herself. She made no more comments on its contents, and my father, Ännchen, and I contented ourselves with eating our dinner.

And so it was arranged. My father was to drive us all to Trenton the next Saturday in time for a picnic lunch with Arnie. We would pack the food with us and pick up

Arnie at the Millers' and then go on to Cadwalader Park and find a picnic table or, if necessary, spread a blanket on the grass. After lunch we would take Arnie back to the Millers' and return to Philadelphia.

I was looking forward to seeing him—I wanted to show off Ännchen to him!

My mother wanted to get a new dress to wear for the occasion and the next morning invited Ännchen to go shopping with her. I think Ännchen was quite surprised at the invitation. Ordinarily, my mother would have brought back a dark garment with a high neckline and a low hemline. This was her customary outfit, made from lighter or heavier material depending on the season. After shopping with Ännchen, however, she brought back a dress that she had to tell my father about.

We were at dinner.

"I thought it was too young for me," she said. "Too close fitting. But Ännchen persuaded me to get it." She wasn't complaining. She had accepted Ännchen's guidance and was happy with the result.

"It is to wear outdoors," Ännchen said to my father. "*Muy guapa!*"

"Well!" my father said. "This ought to be interesting!"

"It's *sturdy* material," my mother said, by way of justification.

"*Muy guapa!*" Ännchen reiterated.

"Ännchen has an eye for clothes," my mother averred. She said to Ännchen, "I'm very grateful to you."

"It was my pleasure, Mrs. Hutlinger."

The dress turned out to be yellow and white and have short sleeves. I couldn't see what the fuss was about. But I was glad to know Ännchen had assisted my mother in a way that she seemed genuinely to appreciate.

One evening that week, after the supper dishes had been washed, dried, and put away, Uncle Claude and Aunt Bett came by the house for a visit. Uncle Claude was my father's older brother. He and Aunt Bett didn't have any children. Aunt Bett had told my mother that she had been "champing at the bit" to meet the new addition to our household ever since she found out that Ännchen had arrived in Philadelphia. This was typical Aunt Bett hyperbole. During the visit, she asked Ännchen, "Are you German or are you Argentinian?" but didn't otherwise single her out to talk to. Aunt Bett always liked to address the entire room, and her favorite topic of conversation was herself. Uncle Claude was cordial, but as was his wont in social situations involving his wife, he let her do all the talking. I was disappointed that they didn't show more interest in Ännchen. For her part, Ännchen betrayed no sign that she found Aunt Bett's conversation to be anything other than delightful (clearly, Ännchen was already a great actress!). Aunt Bett did say one nice thing. When it was time for her and Uncle Claude to leave, she said to Ännchen, "You're a beautiful girl!" That made me feel better.

During the week I started seeing my friends again. My mother insisted. This was fortunate, because otherwise Ännchen would surely have become sick of my company. As it was, we played *Quartett* together every night— in her room sitting on her bed with the door closed and the radio playing. Oddly enough, when I was with one of my friends, I forgot all about her. On Friday I spent the day with my friend Arthur Hambledon, first at his house, then at the zoo accompanied by his mother, then back at his house. Arthur was a classmate of mine. He was almost a year younger than I but far more advanced intellectually (like me, he would go on to the Brinsley School for seventh grade; he would do very well there). At the zoo, he always read the signs that provided information about the animals. I was interested only in looking at the animals, and not for very long either. I think one of the reasons Arthur liked me was that I never complained about what we did or how long it took. If I lost interest in something, I simply zoned out. When we got back to his house, I watched him play with his HO model electric trains. He never seemed to tire of assembling and reassembling the trains in the big railyard set up in his basement. By the time Mrs. Hambledon delivered me to my front door, it was almost suppertime.

And there was Ännchen, coming into the front hall to greet me. She said she had *missed* me! It was a shock. I hadn't thought about her in almost seven hours.

It wasn't that I didn't still love her. I loved her more than ever.

Chapter 9

We made the drive to Trenton in good time and proceeded to the Miller house on Adelaide Avenue, not far from Cadwalader Park. Mrs. Miller answered the door, and my father reintroduced himself and said we were there to pick up Arnie. Mrs. Miller invited us to come in. She didn't hold the door for us but retreated into the hall and asked Ännchen to close the door behind her. We were all standing at the foot of the stairs that led up to the second floor. Mrs. Miller said she hoped we had had a nice drive from Philadelphia. She told my father that having Arnie in the house was a joy and that he was like a second son to her. Such a gentleman! Her own son was up in Canada being a Christian missionary. He was older than Arnie, but she worried on account of him being an unmarried man. Mrs. Miller was afraid he might get engaged to a Canadian girl! She and her husband had only ever seen Canada from Niagara Falls (on their honeymoon trip).

Arnie appeared at the end of the hall and gave us a wave of his hand. He approached Mrs. Miller but made no attempt to get past her. He stood behind her as she continued to talk to my father. This was not an arrangement my mother could endure for long. Mrs. Miller was in the middle of a story about a raccoon on the property that Arnie had tried to scare off when she stepped forward and cut her off.

"Thank you so much," she said to Mrs. Miller. "We so much appreciate your looking after Arnie while he is here in Trenton!" She reached for Arnie's hand and pulled him towards her.

"I'll be back after lunch," Arnie said to Mrs. Miller as he slid around her.

"Enjoy your family!" Mrs. Miller beamed at him.

My mother led Arnie past my father and me and past Ännchen and out the front door. My father told Mrs. Miller it had been delightful meeting her again.

When we were all at the car, parked at the curb, my mother said, "I thought we'd never get away!"

She introduced Arnie to Ännchen. Arnie liked her immediately, as I knew he would. The three of us got into the back seat: Arnie behind my father, I in the middle (over the driveshaft hump), and Ännchen behind my mother. When everyone was seated, my father started the car and pulled away from the curb. My mother began the conversation with Arnie.

She had to turn in her seat to look at him (she couldn't see Ännchen at all). She asked him if Mrs. Miller was as nice as she appeared to be and if he was getting everything he needed. Arnie said that he was being well taken care of and that both Mr. and Mrs. Miller were very good people. She wanted to know if Mrs. Miller did his laundry. Arnie said that she did. They had an automatic washing machine in the basement. Did they have a dryer? No. Mrs. Miller put the clothes out on the line. Was he getting enough to eat? Yes, he certainly was! She said she hadn't expected to see him downstairs when we arrived. Why wasn't he up in his room? Arnie explained that when we arrived, he was having a cup of tea with Mrs. Miller in the kitchen.

It wasn't supposed to be a long drive to Cadwalader Park. But my father seemed to have taken a number of wrong turns trying to get out of the Millers' neighborhood.

"Are we going the right way?" my mother asked, turning her head from Arnie to look ahead of us for a moment.

"We'll get there," said my father.

We moved through the residential streets. My mother told Arnie how pleased we all were to have Ännchen as part of the household.

"She's an adept in the kitchen and never has to have anything explained to her twice. She also gave me advice on selecting my new dress. We went shopping for it together—the one I'm wearing."

"It's a very nice dress, Mother," Arnie said.

"Ännchen came all the way from Argentina by herself! Isn't that so, Ännchen?"

"Yes, Mrs. Hutlinger," said Ännchen, "although Jeanne was very helpful to me in New York."

"*Jeanne.*" My mother emphasized the French pronunciation.

"The girl I stayed with," Ännchen reminded her. "I met her coming from Miami. We sat in the airplane together."

"Did you like New York?" Arnie asked Ännchen.

"Very much. We were in Brooklyn, where Jeanne has her house."

"Her house?" said my mother.

"The house where she lives."

"I'd like to get up to New York," Arnie said. "Did you come out from Penn Station?"

"I did, when I came to Philadelphia. The train made a stop here in Trenton."

"When I was Henry's age, I wanted to be a train conductor. Not the engineer. I wanted to take people's tickets."

"Ännchen wants to be an *actress*," said my mother. It was impossible not to hear the note of disapproval.

"That's true," said Ännchen, not at all abashed.

"You could be on Broadway," said Arnie. "Did you get a chance to see Broadway?"

"I think she has her eye set on Hollywood," said my mother.

This comment caused my father to look at her for a moment. My mother turned in her seat to face forward.

"Are we *lost?*" she said. "Arnie, do you know where we are?"

"We're not *lost*," my father said. He made another turn.

"Well," Arnie said to Ännchen, "Hollywood's another place—if you want to act in movies. There's also television and radio, I guess. Do you have much experience acting?"

"None," said Ännchen.

"None in theater—?"

"None at all."

I chimed in: "I was in the school play."

"What play was that?" said Ännchen.

"*Scenes from William Shakespeare.*"

"You played the soothsayer, didn't you?" said Arnie.

"Uh-huh."

"You never told me you were an actor, Henry!" said Ännchen.

"I only got to say, 'Beware the ides of March!'"

"Acting is all very well," said my mother, who remained facing forward, "but I would worry about following it as a career."

"Someday I'm gonna go out west on the train," said Arnie. "When I do, I'll come to Hollywood and see you."

"That would be nice," Ännchen replied. "I look forward to it!"

I had never been to Trenton before and had no expectation of what Cadwalader Park was going to be like. Doubtless it's not the same now, after all these years (I haven't been back). But when we got there that day, it seemed as though we had entered a magical place. It was still early enough that the park wasn't crowded, and we quickly spotted a nice picnic table in the shade of a grove of trees about a stone's throw from the narrow road. Beyond was an open, sunny field. My father pulled the car over, and we got out and unloaded the lunch supplies and carried them to the table. Ännchen spread out an oilcloth, and soon we were feasting on roast chicken, cornbread, baked macaroni, tuna aspic (awful), cut-up fruit, three-bean salad, and I don't know what else. My mother had made a special dessert called Holiday Mélange that was supposedly a favorite of Arnie's, though I never in my life saw any indication that he particularly liked it. It consisted of green and red cubes of gelatin, crushed pineapple, and slices of banana soaked in lemon juice, all in a white matrix of marshmallow fluff topped off with red rubyettes.

My father had just finished his own serving of the dessert when he asked Arnie, "Can you tell me, without revealing names or any privileged information, what it is you are doing that requires you to take your work back to the Millers'?"

"It's the interrogatories," Arnie said. "And the transcripts of the depositions. There are pages and pages. We have to go through all of them to find any mention of certain alleged facts. Any mention of letters or conversations or actions that may have taken place involving different people. It's a lot of work. Mr. Finback said it's called discovery."

"That's right."

"The stuff is delivered to the office by the boxload. Mr. Finback knows I've been taking the boxes home—I mean to the Millers'."

"Well, that's what you get working for a litigator."

"Have you done much of that kind of work, Dad?"

"I haven't. If a client needs to bring a lawsuit, I refer him to someone like Gus. Just remember, there are different kinds of lawyer. Gus is a *litigator*. I'm a *facilitator*. Trusts and wills; conveyancing and contracts—"

"I think a facilitator is more the kind of lawyer I'd rather be."

"We'll see." This statement did not sound like a ringing vote of confidence.

My mother, who had been listening to the conversation, was frowning.

Arnie said to Ännchen, "When did you decide you wanted to become an actress?"

Ännchen considered the question.

"There was not just one moment when I decided. I went to see motion pictures starting from an early age, when I was thirteen years old. Many girls want to become an actress at some time. But with me the desire only grew."

"What did your parents think about it?"

"My mother was not encouraging. But I would remind her that Evita was an actress. She came from poverty and worked hard and became an actress."

"Who is she—?"

"She was the wife of the *presidente* of Argentina. She was an actress before her marriage. Unfortunately, she died."

"Oh, I'm sorry!"

"She died at thirty-three years. It was very sad. We're not supposed to talk about it."

"Why not?"

"It is an offense to mention her name."

"To mention her *name?*"

"Under the current government of my country." Ännchen shook her head.

"But you say you haven't done any acting yet?"

"I have not. But I was a model for clothes. I know how to dress and how to walk. That's more important than you might think. And I'm able to speak in front of people."

"That's essential in the courtroom," said my father.

"You can become a good speaker," Ännchen went on, "just from reading aloud to your family. I read stories and articles from the newspapers to my mother and father. My mother never liked to. When she read aloud, she sounded like a seven-year-old child!"

This characterization of her own mother sounded a bit harsh.

My mother said, "I'm sure she is a very worthy person."

"She is," said Ännchen. "I owe everything to my mother."

"Speaking of mothers, Mother," said Arnie, "the lunch was delicious. Thank you for making it."

My mother smiled.

"You must thank Ännchen as well," she said.

"Thank you, Ännchen."

"It was a pleasure, Arnie."

"But I think I ate too much! I need to walk around. Would you like to come for a stroll?" He was asking Ännchen.

"Very much," she said.

She and Arnie got up from the table. Arnie looked at me.

"You, too, sport!"

"Don't wander too far," my mother said.

The three of us headed towards the open field. We hadn't walked into it very far when we stopped.

"Maybe I should become an actor," Arnie said. He was looking out across the grass.

"I'm going to become an actor, too," I said.

"Your father wants you to be a lawyer," Ännchen said to Arnie.

"Dad wants me to be a lawyer," Arnie confirmed. "Only he doesn't think I have it in me. He may be right."

"What will you do?"

"Keep trying, I suppose."

"Arnie, will you let me tell you one thing?"

"What?"

"You shouldn't live to please them."

"Them?"

"Either of them. You must follow your own path."

Arnie didn't say anything. I guess he was considering what she had said.

"Your life belongs to you. To no one else." Ännchen then addressed me. "Henry, do you see that sculpture over there?" She pointed across the field to where there was a statue atop a massive pedestal. The statue appeared to be of a man sitting in a chair.

"It looks like some guy in a chair," I said.

"Do you know who he is?"

"No."

"Is there a way to find out? The name must be written in the stone."

"You want me to go read it?" I was all set to run across the field.

"Wait!" Ännchen produced a white cloth handkerchief from somewhere on her person. "Take this. When you get there, wave it so that we can see you! If there is writing, read what it says."

I took the handkerchief and ran. I should have walked. The sprint itself just about winded me, and when I got to the statue I turned around and began to jump up and down and wave the handkerchief like a man possessed. Arnie and Ännchen had shrunk to two small figures in a sea of green. They waved back at me. Farther back were my parents, sitting at the picnic table. They waved, too.

Finally, I stopped my jumping and waving and stood still to catch my breath. It looked as though Arnie and Ännchen were talking to each other. Ännchen was shaking her head. As I watched them, I realized that what I really wanted was for Arnie to marry Ännchen. I knew I was too young for her, but Arnie wasn't, and there was no more deserving person in the world than he. If he married Ännchen, she wouldn't have to go to Hollywood. She wouldn't have to leave us!

The inscription on the pedestal of the statue awaited my scrutiny. It was quite long and included not only the man's name—John A. Roebling—but also his accomplishments, one of which was the building of suspension bridges. After committing as much of the information as I could to memory, I ran back across the field towards where Arnie and Ännchen were waiting. About thirty feet short of reaching them, I stumbled and fell hard onto the grass. Arnie and Ännchen came forward to help me up.

"Whoa, sport!" said Arnie, holding me by my arm.

"*Pobrecito!*" Ännchen smoothed out my clothes with her hands. Then she fixed my hair.

"I'm all right!" I said, elated and wheezing.

I told them what I had learned about Mr. Roebling.

Chapter 10

The next day was Sunday. At breakfast my father told me that when I was finished I needed to get ready for church. He and I were going to go to services together, he said, just the two of us. I couldn't believe it. None of us had ever gone to church without my mother. I said I didn't want to go if we weren't all going. My mother said that my father had been wanting to take me to church for a long time (this was not true) and that I should be very pleased. I looked at Ännchen. She just smiled as though she was happy for me.

I don't think she was any more aware of what was going on than I was. The truth was that I was being taken away so that my mother could have a private talk with her. My mother wanted to talk to her about the woman from Brooklyn named Jeanne that Ännchen had stayed with for six days before coming to Philadelphia. The woman had pricked my mother's interest. So while I sat on a pew with my father at the Gethsemane Lutheran Church, zoning out from boredom, Ännchen contended with questions from my mother about Jeanne. My mother found out that Jeanne was a regular visitor to Miami, that she usually made the trip during the winter months, but sometimes later in the year as well. More to the point, she found out that Jeanne did not travel with her husband, because she had no husband. For my mother, the implication was clear: the woman was a good-time girl if not an actual prostitute. Ännchen neither confirmed nor denied this conjecture. She said only that she was grateful to Jeanne for letting her stay with her in Brooklyn while she waited for her father's bank cable and for helping her set up an account at the Hanover Bank.

My mother told Ännchen she thought her decision to accept Jeanne's hospitality showed very poor judgment. She didn't give this as the reason for her insistence that Ännchen leave our house, however. What she said to my father was that she could no longer *trust* Ännchen. For it turned out that Ännchen had not been truthful about her age. In the course of their conversation, she admitted to my mother that she was not in fact eighteen as she had earlier claimed, but twenty-three.

When I learned about all this (again, from Arnie and a long time afterwards), I was dumbfounded. Why, I wondered, would anyone care that Ännchen had lied about her age? On the platform at Thirtieth Street Station, my mother had told her that we had been expecting a fourteen-year-old. She must have detected my mother's disappointment that she was older. So what did she do? She narrowed the gap a little and gave her age as eighteen.

Hardly a capital offense. But my mother was adamant. Ännchen had to go—and quick, too.

I can't imagine that Ännchen felt that this harsh treatment was justified. But she made no protest when, sometime after Sunday dinner, my father told her that it was time for her to move on (or however he put it to her). He said he had talked to Mr. Falkenstein, who was arranging for her temporary accommodation at a Philadelphia hotel. Mr. Falkenstein would be coming to the house for her early the next morning. Ännchen's only request was that she be allowed to say good-bye to me.

Perhaps she had been expecting such a dismissal. My mother had never warmed up to her. I think, though, that everything would have been all right for at least a little while longer if it hadn't been for the visit to see Arnie in Trenton. Arnie was my mother's fair-haired boy, and it was pretty clear that when he met Ännchen he found her to be a charming and attractive young woman. After the picnic, when we were dropping Arnie off at the Millers', he told Ännchen that he was looking forward to seeing her again when he came home for a visit, whenever that might be. "Well, of *course* you are," said my mother, as though Arnie was making a fuss over nothing. This was maternal jealousy speaking, I'm sure of it.

Ännchen came to my room Sunday night after I was in bed with the lights out. She was in her nightgown. Up to this point, I had had no inkling that anything was amiss. Earlier in the evening we had played our usual game of *Quartett* on her bed with the door closed and the radio playing. She had been her usual self.

"Henry," she said. She sat down on the edge of my bed, taking care not to sit on my legs. I was lying on my back with the covers pulled up to my chin. She was a dusky figure in blue, but there was enough light coming in from the hallway for me to see her face. "It is time for me to go."

"Go where?"

"Away. Tomorrow early. I want to say good-bye."

"Are you coming back?"

She shook her head.

"You mean you're not gonna live in our house anymore?"

"No."

I could feel my chest tighten.

"You knew I had to leave sometime," she said.

"I thought you were going to be here all summer! I haven't even gone to *camp* yet!"

"*Liebling*—my life is calling me. I must go when and where it calls."

"That's stupid!"

"Don't say that, Henry."

"Where you gonna go?"

"New York. Then Los Angeles."

"You mean Hollywood?"

"Yes."

I took it as a given that she would start acting in feature movies immediately upon her arrival there. She told me once that all she needed to do was get a screen test (whatever that was).

"Will I ever see you again?" I asked.

"I don't know." It was a muted reply.

I turned my face away from her. I was afraid I was going to cry.

"I'll write to you if you want me to," she said.

I didn't respond to this.

"Or if you don't want me to, I won't."

I still didn't respond.

"Perhaps you'll see me in a *movie!*" This was an attempt to strike a cheery note.

"I hate movies," I said.

"No, you don't."

"Yes, I do."

Ännchen cupped her hand over a bump in the blanket where one of my knees was, and for a time neither of us spoke.

"We've been good friends, no?" she said at last.

"Uh-huh."

"And you're going to have more good friends."

"No, I'm not."

"And someday you'll marry."

"No, I won't."

"Someday you'll marry, and it will be a wonder!"

"No, it won't."

"Will you let me kiss you good-bye?"

I didn't respond. I was keeping my face turned away from her. She scooched up the bed.

"Give me your hand," she said.

I removed my right hand from under the covers, and she took it into her own and held it. Then, with her other hand, she turned my face towards her and, leaning down and tilting her head the way they do in the movies, kissed me on the lips. It was not the kind of kiss I was used to, which up to that point had only been the peck-on-the-cheek kind from people like Aunt Bett. When the kiss was over, Ännchen straightened back up.

I said, "You'll forget me."

She thought for a moment.

"Will you give me something of yours to remind me?" She was still holding my hand.

"What?"

"The little man on the shelf? The little sitting man!"

The idol did not belong to me. It was part of my father's porcelain collection.

I took my hand from hers and raised myself onto my elbows.

"Wait here!"

She scooched back down the bed, and I got out from under the covers. Then, in my pajamas, I crept out of the room and down the hallway. My parents were in their bedroom with the door closed. Stepping carefully, I descended the stairs and went to the mantelpiece in the living room.

When I had the idol secure in my hand, I examined it in the dim light coming from the front hall. Did the grotesque little Billiken really look like me—the large head and stomach, the stubby little arms and legs, the oversized feet and toes with the undersides so prominently displayed? The first time Ännchen saw it, she had laughed and said it reminded her of me. I returned to my room.

"Here it is," I said, giving the idol to Ännchen. She was still sitting on the bed. Once again, she laughed to look at the creature.

"Thank you, Henry."

"You're welcome."

"I'll keep it with me always. I'll think of you whenever I look at it and remember how nice you are."

"OK."

"But what will your father do—when he sees that it is gone from its place on the shelf?"

"I'll tell him I broke it by accident and that I was afraid he'd get mad so I threw the pieces away."

"You're a clever boy!"

I grinned.

"It will be our secret!" she said.

I got back into bed and lay down and pulled the covers back up to my chin. Ännchen scooched up near me again.

Her brow contracted into a frown.

"I don't want you to get up and see me in the morning. Mr. Falkenstein is coming for me tomorrow early. Will you promise not to get up?"

"Can't I say good-bye to you?"

"I don't want you to."

"Why?"

"It will make me too sad."

I didn't say anything more.

"Will you promise not to get up, until I'm away?"

I nodded.

She gave me another kiss, this time the peck-on-the-cheek kind. She waited a moment before rising from the bed. Then, moving slowly and holding on to the idol, she left the room.

She had been with us a total of eleven days.

Epilogue

Arnie more or less defied my father when he decided not to try to get into law school.

After he graduated from college, he enlisted in the Army. He was in for three years and attained the rank of "spec 4" (specialist 4), which is about equivalent to the rank of corporal. As an army volunteer, he had the choice of which geographical area to serve in, and he chose Europe. His assignment was to the Military Pay Office in Frankfurt, West Germany. He liked the posting and was good at the job, which was essentially that of secretary. After his three years were up, he received his discharge and returned to Philadelphia and got a job as a teller at a bank. Neither of my parents was especially pleased with this choice of occupation, but at least it was white collar and the job was in Philadelphia (there had been some talk about his going out to Washington state, where an army friend of his was from, and working as a forester!). He never became a big earner. I was already making more money than he was when I began work as an insurance adjuster.

But the joke was on us. Arnie is a happy person. He married a delightful girl named Jackie Fisher, a commercial fashion artist in Philadelphia, and they're still together. I've been married and divorced twice. Arnie and Jackie never had any children of their own, but they were like a second set of parents to my daughter, Isabel, especially after my divorce from her mother (Isabel was all of thirteen when that happened). They also dote on Teddy, my young grandson. Arnie has been my rock all my life. He visits me at least once a week here at the "home," and Jackie often comes with him and brings me books and movies and other things she thinks I need.

I'm not in the best of health anymore, which is why last August I made the move to Sablehaven Senior Living ("Make your next move to Sablehaven!" is the tagline in the ad). Isabel, devoted daughter that she is, wanted me to come live with her and Teddy. But she's a single mom, and I didn't think adding to her responsibilities that way would be doing either of us a favor.

Sablehaven's not a bad place. The food is decent and the coffee good, and I have my own room and access to all my things. They don't allow dogs or cats, but you can have a canary or parakeet if you are able to keep it confined in its cage (I don't have a bird myself; I also don't *want* one, as I had to explain to Isabel and Jackie). I only ever leave the premises when Arnie or Isabel takes me to see the doctor or home to one or the other of their houses to have dinner. They take good care of me.

I never found out whether Ännchen became an actress. If she had any career to speak of, she must have changed her name. In almost sixty years of reading movie and television credits, I've never seen the name Anna Maria Eichenbogen roll by. One time I thought I saw her face on an episode of *Perry Mason*—but I was probably deluding myself. It would have been in an uncredited role. For three months during my freshman year at BU, I subscribed to the *Hollywood Reporter* in hopes of coming across some mention of her. There was nothing. She never wrote to me, and it seems Mr. Falkenstein lost track of her soon after she left Philadelphia for New York. He was not able to confirm that she had gone on to Los Angeles. At this late date, I have to wonder whether she's still living.

I remember the morning she left us. As soon as I awoke, I went to her room, still in my pajamas. She was gone. The bed was neatly made with the bedspread pulled up over the pillow, and the radio was in its place on the table desk. But all her own things had vanished: the combs, brushes, containers, and bottles, the framed photograph of herself, the movie magazines, the juvenile novel in German she was reading (*Inge muss in die Welt*, it was called—the pages were printed in Fraktur), the big sketch pad containing her drawings of women wearing chic-looking clothing (as it seemed to me), the pens and pencils, the travel alarm clock that collapsed into its own little case. No trace of her remained, not even a stray hair or a speck of powder on top of the chest of drawers.

I don't know how long I stood there looking. Eventually I crept back to my own room. There I discovered that she had left something after all. On my bedside table was the deck of cards she and I had used to play *Quartett*, the game where you tried to get four of the same kind of marine animal. She must have placed the cards there early that morning while I slept. I picked them up and turned them over. The card on the bottom of the deck was a starfish—*der Seestern*. The picture showed the creature resting comfortably on the sea floor surrounded by minnows. But such was my state of mind that I hardly knew what I was looking at. Nothing at that moment seemed real to me, not even my own body.

At breakfast I barely touched my food. There was no mention by my parents of Ännchen or of Mr. Falkenstein, and I didn't ask any questions. The rest of the morning I spent moving from inside the house to the back yard and from the back yard to inside the house, just to be doing something. Finally, my mother felt my forehead and put me to bed. When she took my temperature with the thermometer, she got a reading of 101.

I was in bed for four days, and there was some doubt as to whether I would be able to attend Camp Mon-Su-Ming-Nee. But by Friday it seemed as though I had recovered from whatever it was that was afflicting me, and I was adjudged fit to go. Fit or not fit (I would have said *not fit*), I was on the camp bus when it left for the Poconos the next morning.

Looking back, I'm glad I went. Contrary to my feeling that I would never be able to enjoy anything again, I had a pretty good three weeks. I learned how to paddle a canoe using the J-stroke and attained the rank of Junior Pathfinder, an honorific that came with a neat little penknife.

The penknife is long gone, but I still have the *Quartett* cards. For years I held on to them with a kind of mulish devotion. Their place of honor was just inside my bed-side-table drawer. I hardly ever got them out—I just liked having them near me. They were still there when I went away to college and still there when I graduated and went to work. Then when I got engaged to Janet, Isabel's mother, I cleared the drawer out and put the contents in a cardboard box that I was filling with stuff to be taken up to my parents' attic. It seemed like the appropriate thing to do (Janet and I wanted the table).

That cardboard box is now on the shelf in my closet here at Sablehaven. Besides the *Quartett* cards, it contains my student card from BU, an address book, a fold-up map of Boston with an MBTA subway ticket clipped to it, a Parker House ashtray, a 1964 wall calendar from Ming's Famous Flower Chinese Restaurant, a shaving kit, a stainless-steel lighter, Pam O'Dwyer's *garter* that I caught at Pam and Peedee's wedding, a plastic back scratcher, an ocarina, a rubber stamp that imprints the words "Student Study Group A," a Kodak Instamatic camera, and a jumble of loose photographs, negatives, beer coasters, and receipts—all artifacts from my college days (and the period of my first deferment; later I would get a medical exemption for asthma). The address book only has about fifteen or twenty names and addresses written in it, and I don't think I've seen or communicated with any of those people since that time. Valerie, my second wife, told me I was a pack rat. These days she'd probably call me a hoarder.

I really should pass the *Quartett* cards on to young Teddy. Isabel can help him identify the sea creatures, though you don't have to know their names to play the game. The two of them will be coming over next week along with Arnie and Jackie Fisher as my guests for dinner in the dining room, and I can give the cards to Teddy then—if Isabel will permit it. My daughter can get sentimental about these things. "I don't want you to be deprived of them," she'll say. I'll tell her, "It's all right, I've held on to them long enough." "No," she'll say, "we need to keep the cards *here* so that we can play the game with you when we visit." She's a bit of a manager that way. Sentimental, but *practical.*

I'm looking forward to seeing them all.

The Way He Met Her

It was a weekend in early spring, and Parkman, age thirty-three, was a visitor at the Western Eastern Open, a chess tournament that was being held in one of the tall office buildings in downtown Clayton.

It was an unusual venue. The tournament hall was right at the top of the building, in a kind of super-added atrium of plate glass in the shape of an arch. This grandiose enclosure looked out in all directions over St. Louis County and City and let in so much daylight that it hurt your eyes to look up from your game. The playing area was located away from the elevators on the far side of a wall of potted plants that divided the hall in two. On the near side you could get something to eat and drink and socialize. Some of the games from round one had already been completed by the time Parkman arrived, and the first thing he noticed on getting out of the elevator was a group of people gathered around a pile of cardboard boxes. Someone was in the process of breaking the boxes down. Parkman went over.

He asked a young man who was holding a cup of coffee what was going on. The young man said that there was a party of three Russians in attendance at the tournament and that they had just been challenged by a kid from one of the local high schools to a game of a variant form of chess called Leningrad. Parkman had never heard of Leningrad. It was new and came out of Russia, the young man said. There had already been some notable matches in Europe at the Grandmaster level, and so far the Russians had proved insuperable.

Parkman listened carefully as the rules were explained to him. As challenger, the local high-school kid would be playing the white pieces minus the pawns and queen. White's starting position was a piece on every other square on the two adjoining sides of the board that met at the white square in the corner. That square was occupied by the white king. Nearest to the king, on either side, were placed the knights, then the rooks, then the bishops. As defender, the three Russians (who were playing as a team) would be playing the black pieces with just the king and pawns. Black's starting position was in the 3 x 3 box in the corner opposite to White. The black king faced the white king on the long diagonal with the black pawns massed in front of it. The moves of the pieces were the same as in classical chess, except that 1) Black's pawns could advance only one square, not two, on their initial moves and 2) they could move and capture "forward" in two directions, towards either edge of the board where White was set up. As in classical chess, the pawns could be promoted. White won the game by checkmating the black king within twenty moves. If White failed to checkmate within twenty moves, Black won. Black could also win by checkmating the white king. The only draw permitted was a stalemate.

These were the rules of the board. To make matters more interesting, however, the challenger had to meet a special requirement: he must design and build, on the spot and using materials at hand, a kind of *glider* capable of holding himself and the defender, which he must "fly" (sliding off the top of the office building!) and land safely somewhere, all the while playing his own side of the game on the chessboard. The challenger was allowed to have help in the construction of the craft, and the Russians very good-naturedly pitched in. Parkman himself assisted a little, though at this stage he mostly stood and watched. What he saw both fascinated and disturbed him.

The craft was built quickly, in less than half an hour. It consisted of a framework of 1 x 2 wooden slats covered over with cardboard (from the boxes that Parkman had seen being broken down when he arrived). In the cockpit there was a yoke or "steering wheel," also made of the 1 x 2s, very unskillfully nailed together (it looked like a fixture from a kid's tree house). There were no other visible controls or instruments. Yet the interior of the cabin looked remarkably authentic, with actual seats and windows. If you squinted your eyes a little, you might have thought you were inside a shrunk-down Douglas DC-2, the kind of airplane that was featured in the movie *Lost Horizon* (1937 version). The wings of the craft, however, didn't look quite right. They looked too short, and rather than being fixed into a horizontal position relative to the fuselage, they were fixed into more of a V shape, like the upward-spread wings of the eagle in the old American Airlines logo. Only this was no eagle. The craft did not inspire confidence, not in Parkman. Moreover, it was going to be piloted by a totally inexperienced fifteen-year-old high-school kid after being pushed off the top of a tall office building in the middle of a large city.

This wasn't the worst of it, however. Another requirement of the game was that the craft carry passengers. Six to eight passengers, in addition to the actual chess players, just to put an added burden on the challenger. The kid asked for volunteers, and, to Parkman's amazement, several people came forward and climbed into the craft.

"Anyone else?" The kid was looking at Parkman.

One of the things Parkman had been living with for years was the idea in his family that he was a stick-in-the-mud. He liked chess, for example, but he only ever played over the board. He never played on line. He also never played any of those frenetic computer games that his younger brother, Matty, liked to play (Matty, at thirty years old, was a dedicated "gamer"). And now here was a completely novel experience beckoning to him. Was Parkman a stick-in-the-mud? He didn't like to think so. He stepped forward and got into the craft.

He located an unoccupied seat next to a young woman with straw-colored hair who was sitting at the back where there were two seats together. When Parkman asked, "Is this seat taken?" meaning the seat next to her, the young woman looked up and smiled and slowly shook her head. Parkman couldn't help noticing her pretty eyes. They were sea blue and twinkled behind a pair of thick, harlequin-frame glasses. He smiled back and took his seat.

In due course, the craft was pushed to an open, double-wide service door, through which it was carefully maneuvered to the edge of an outside catwalk. Now the craft was ready to be launched. It began to tip—and suddenly they were away! Parkman experienced that sickening falling sensation where your stomach rises in your body. Then, somehow, the craft caught a flow of air and began to stabilize. There were nervous little chuckles of relief from the passengers. Parkman could see out the window that the craft was in fact "gliding," albeit at a very steep angle and at what seemed like accelerating speed. He looked at the young pilot, who was busy at the steering wheel (he was wearing a white T-shirt), steady and cool and concentrating hard. He had no chance at all to play the actual chess game with his three Russian opponents. Gathered just behind him in the cockpit, they were content to sit quietly by and watch him steer. It was no wonder the Russians had won every match they had played so far. This was because they never played the side of challenger!

Parkman thought the kid did a creditable job. He brought the glider—most of it, at least—successfully to the ground at a location not well suited to a landing. It was a rail line, the new Metrolink cross-county extension. Built for trains running on electricity, the line was overstrung by power cables, and when the craft came down onto them, it bounced once or twice and then began to skid along them. This action resulted very quickly in the wings of the craft being sheared off from the fuselage, at which point the fuselage plopped down onto the rails.

It wasn't a graceful landing, to be sure, but it was a landing nonetheless. The only problem was that the now-wingless craft had come to rest in what appeared to be the path of an oncoming train. The headlight from the train was shining into the cabin through the cockpit windows, and when Parkman and his fellow passengers became aware of this—well, you can imagine their reaction. Everyone became very alarmed. There was a scream, and the next thing Parkman knew, he was locked in a fearful embrace with the young woman with the straw-colored hair. They clung to each other for what they thought were their last moments on earth. But fortune was smiling on them, because the train lumbered by on an adjoining track, missing the craft completely.

Afterwards, when it was all over, Parkman's new friend—her name was *Julie*—shook her head and said that they must have been seated next to each other "on purpose" (i.e., providentially) just in case such a scary thing happened. Parkman could only agree with her. "I felt it from the moment I sat down," he said. She looked at him, and her pretty sea-blue eyes began to twinkle behind her thick, harlequin-frame glasses.

Out of the Burrow

We had been living on our scrubby hillside for as long as anyone could remember. Admittedly, our memories didn't go very far back, but we never forgot that everything within foraging range of our village belonged to *us* and to no one else. If your alert lorpa got so much as a whiff of a prairie dog, he or she became the most agitated creature on earth. Intruders would be dealt with!

Of course, we still had our natural predators—hawks, owls, snakes, coyotes, big cats, weasels, foxes, badgers. This was why we lived in the village. In the village, there were always lorpas on sentry duty keeping an eye out. The moment a hawk was spotted in the sky, alarm-chirps would begin sounding all over town. The alarm-chirp was your signal to get yourself home to your burrow as fast as possible. If you didn't think you could make it in time—if, for example, you had wandered very far down towards the plain in search of food—you hid under a bush and hoped for the best. Eventually the danger would pass, and you could come out again.

It might be supposed that, living all together as we did, we were used to getting along with one another. We were *sociable*, yes. We were acquainted with our neighbors (the near ones, at least), and some of us, especially the young among us, had friends. But our sociability was limited—or should I say *volatile*. The problem was the lorpa temper. My mother once became downright ferocious with Mrs. Chew, who lived across the way, just because, during a conversation they were having, Mrs. Chew began to ferret-dance in front of her. My mother's reaction was to rake Mrs. Chew across the face with her claws. There was an awful scene, and afterwards the two wouldn't speak to each other. "She disrespected me," my mother explained.

You really could go almost anywhere in our village and come across an altercation in progress. The point at issue might be a piece of food, where someone was digging, who had the right of way along a path—or, indeed, some mysterious act of "disrespect." The saving grace was that if fighting broke out, with claws catching and biting, it usually lasted but a few moments. Very quickly, one of the parties would disengage and slink away to lick his or her wounds. For my part, I didn't like getting scratched up one bit. I discovered this truth about myself after reaching adolescence, when playing with friends suddenly became a much rougher proposition. "Augie," my mother would say, "go outside and play with your friends!" And I would try to find something else to do.

I was an oddball. Less gregarious than other lorpas, I really had only one friend, and that was Dylan, who was even more of an oddball than I was. We both had the same problem, which was that we were incompetent. We were poor hunters and unenthusiastic diggers and never seemed able to perform up to expectations. But we enjoyed each other's company. Then one day Dylan got ejected from his home. If a young male lorpa stayed long enough at home, if he didn't leave before he reached a certain stage of maturity, one of two things happened. Either his father ejected him from the burrow or, less often, he ejected his father and became de facto head of the family. In either case the ejection was swift, violent, and permanent. Father and son never spoke to each other again. Poor old Dylan was sent packing. At the time I had no idea what had happened. Dylan had simply vanished, and no one would say anything. Finally, one afternoon I heard him calling my name down our burrow hole. "Augie—Augie!" I scrambled up to the surface and found him crouching behind a bitten-down tuft of grass.

He told me he was living down the hillside, outside the village. He was living on the outside, he said, to keep his distance from his father. I couldn't believe how thin he looked. What was he getting to eat? Mostly fresh spring shoots and pill bugs, he said. Shifting for yourself wasn't so bad if you didn't mind fresh spring shoots and pill bugs, ha, ha! That was Dylan. Always cheerful. He promised to come back for another visit when he got more settled. But he never did come back.

Seeing Dylan, I couldn't help thinking about my own future. My two older brothers, Buddy and Scooter, had already left home of their own accord and had found wives and started families. Only my younger sister, Contessa, and I remained. How much longer would it be before I had to leave—or be thrown out?

Chapter 2

Our village covered a large swath of hillside and was divided into neighborhoods. There was the Far End, Lower Village, Upper Village, and Knobville. The neighborhoods functioned practically like villages in themselves. Each posted its own sentries and, with the exception of Knobville, maintained a sizeable population. Each neighborhood also had its own characteristics. In the Far End, where my family lived, everything was kept in good order. We kept not only our burrows tidy but also the network of dirt paths at the surface. Stray pebbles were rolled away, so that running the paths was always quick and easy. "We have pride of place in the Far End," my mother said. It was the natural result of the fact that only the best kind lived in the Far End—an opinion shared by all our Far End neighbors. Outsiders, or "undesirables," were not welcome. If you were from outside the neighborhood, you were likely to get chased off. Even if you were *from* the Far End, you weren't immune from harassment. It was expected that when out in public, away from your burrow, you attend to your business. If you didn't move along quickly, if you lingered or loitered too long near someone else's burrow, a head would pop out of the ground and snarl at you. This, too, was part of pride of place.

Lower Village, where Dylan was from, was different. It was situated on the lower hillside and was as messy and disorderly as the Far End was neat and tidy. The burrows were carelessly dug, with dirt and gravel flung out just any old way, plus there were many shallow holes where digging had been abandoned for one reason or another, making it hard to tell where the real burrows were. The inhabitants of Lower Village did not have pride of place.

One advantage of this was that you were much less likely to get chased off if you were from outside the neighborhood. Dylan and I used to run all over Lower Village. Our favorite place to go was a lone-standing pine tree just beyond the village edge. We would pretend we were tree squirrels and try to run up the tree trunk to see who could get the highest before falling back to earth. Neither of us was wont to venture very far down towards the plain. It was safer to stay close to the village.

But now my friend had gone away. Dylan had been ejected from his home and had gone to live on his own. He had told me he was living outside the village to keep his distance from his father. I could understand his desire not to risk an encounter with the one who had ejected him. But I had no idea where he was—no idea where in the vastness of the wild country he had hidden himself. I would have liked to be able to see him again.

It was clear to me that it was only a matter of time before I, too, would have to go live on my own. It was also clear to me that if I didn't undertake the move myself, my father would do to me what Dylan's father had done to Dylan. That much was a certainty. But I had no plan for leaving home, no plan at all. Feckless creature that I was, I felt there was nothing to do but wait for the blow to fall.

And it was looking like the blow was going to fall soon, too. The first thing that happened was that my father started to body-bump me. If he was passing anywhere near me on his way into or out of the burrow, he would make a sudden diversion and bump me with the side of his body. It wasn't a hard bump, but he did it so quickly that I was almost always unprepared.

A more powerful signal came when both he and my mother stopped sharing food with me. Nothing was said.

They simply ceased to leave anything over for me to eat at mealtimes. I would have gone hungry if it hadn't been for Contessa. Unlike me, my sister was an excellent hunter (for a lorpa) and did her best to make sure I got something. Then my father started to *growl* at me. He had stopped the body-bumping, which was a relief, but if I got too near him, he would emit a low growl. He also stopped speaking to me. If he and I both happened to be above ground, he would just stare. This unnerved me so much that I began to spend more time away from the burrow.

Where I went was Lower Village. I had been to Dylan's burrow in Lower Village many times in the past (to the entrance, to call for Dylan), and my visits had always been tolerated well enough by his family. Dylan's older sister, Queenie, even liked me. But now that Dylan no longer lived there, I avoided the area. I would wander aimlessly around other parts of the neighborhood, making my way eventually to the tree where Dylan and I used to frolic. I would crouch in the shade and look out over the plain till the sun set. I suppose I was hoping that Dylan might return to our old haunt. But it seemed he had permanently exiled himself. When I got back home, I would go to my room and wait for Contessa to visit. She would come with food for me.

One morning as I was making my way along one of the paths in Lower Village, I had a chance encounter with Dylan's father. We were traveling in opposite directions and almost collided. I managed to dodge him by jumping off the path, but not before he tried to cuff me with his paw. He turned on me, and I could see him curl his lip and bare his teeth. He was ready to pounce. Then he recognized me.

"You're Augie!" he said.

"Yes, sir."

"Well, well! Come out of the grass so I can get a look at you."

I crawled back onto the path.

"You're all grown up!"

"Yes, sir."

"We haven't seen you in a long time, Augie! You know, Queenie was asking about you."

"I hope she's doing well, sir."

"She's doing very well. She's a fine female creature, Augie! One of these days, she's going to make somebody a fine wife."

"Yes, sir." I was just being polite. According to Dylan, Queenie was extremely lazy and hardly ever emerged from the burrow except maybe to go out and nibble on spring grass (a not over-strenuous activity). She was bossy, too. She bossed everyone, including her father.

"Where have you been keeping yourself?"

"At home."

"At home? You mean with your folks?"

"Yes, sir."

It took Dylan's father a moment to assess the significance of this information. Suddenly his brow contracted.

"Now, you listen to me. You go out and find yourself a nice patch of dirt and dig yourself a burrow. Your *own* burrow."

"Me?"

"Yes, you. Do it! You had better!"

I didn't know what to say.

"You know how to dig a *burrow*, don't you?" I thought he was going to cuff me one. But he didn't. He continued to give me instructions: "Now, after you get yourself a place to live—after you dig your *own* burrow—

come around and see us! Do you understand what I'm telling you?"

"Yes, sir!"

"Your *own* burrow!"

He shook his head and moved on. I thought I heard him mutter something under his breath.

No one had given me advice like this before. Certainly not my father. In my family, it was assumed that you knew what you were supposed to do instinctively. To be sure, Contessa had tried to teach me hunting skills; but even she got exasperated with my slow progress. And now here was someone from outside the family, someone who had ejected his own son from the burrow, giving me advice on what I had better do. I marveled at his going to the trouble. Of course, he was right. It would make sense to have a burrow ready for the time when I had to leave home. Or did he mean I should start digging *now* and move in as soon as possible? Could it be that he was trying to save me from the fate of his son?

Chapter 3

I decided to get to work that very morning.

The only question was, where? I ruled out my own neighborhood. If I started digging in the Far End, my father would find out very quickly what I was up to, and I had no idea how he would react. He was already hostile. Besides, opening up a new burrow in the Far End was almost always met by opposition from neighbors. You had to be prepared to fight them off. Both my brothers, Buddy and Scooter, had had to fight neighbors when they were digging there.

Upper Village was a possibility. It was a perfectly respectable sort of place and in many ways very nice. The best views of the plain were to be had from Upper Village, for which reason the neighborhood was considered the safest as far as four-legged predators were concerned (the ones that prowled during the day, at least). But there was the problem with the rocks. The higher up the hillside you went, the rockier the soil became and the harder it was to dig.

That left Lower Village, where the digging was easy ("*too* easy," I can hear my mother saying). Best of all, nothing I did there was likely to attract anyone's attention—certainly not my father's. I would, just to be on the safe side, steer clear of the area where Dylan's family lived. No need for Dylan's father—or Queenie—to know where I was relocating (in my "*own* burrow"). I didn't even consider Knobville. It was the oldest part of town and pretty much excavated to capacity. Knobville was also the neighborhood my mother mentioned more than any other as being populated by "undesirables." I had always avoided it.

The site I chose was off the beaten track, in an area where there had been little previous excavation. It would have been easy enough to take over an existing, abandoned hole—there were plenty to choose from in Lower Village—but I wanted to dig from scratch. Digging from scratch meant that no one would be able to come along later and claim ownership because his great-granduncle Fescue, or whoever, had dug there first. Not that there was much chance of that happening in Lower Village. But there was no harm in being careful.

I certainly wasn't the world's most expert excavator, but as I got to work, I felt a sense of purpose that spurred me on. By early afternoon, I had the entrance tunnel dug and had begun on the main chamber. And I didn't just kick the dirt away, Lower Village–style. I used it to build a half-ring pile around the uphill side of the hole. This was the way it was done in the Far End, and I saw no reason to do it differently just because I was digging somewhere else. The half-ring pile served to shield the hole from runoff rainwater.

Every so often I took a break to assess my progress. It was during one of these breaks, while I was standing outside the hole, that I was surprised by an unfamiliar voice.

"Hi!"

I turned, and there, not four hops away and crouching, was a young male lorpa. He was so young that he didn't know to be afraid to address a stranger.

"Whatcha doing?" he said.

"I'm digging a burrow."

"My name's Baxter."

I cast a quick glance around the vicinity. The young one appeared to be by himself.

"Why're you diggin' a burrow?" he said.

"To live in."

I went down the hole. When I came back out a moment later, Baxter said, "*We* got a burrow."

"You better get yourself home before your parents come looking for you."

Baxter was unconcerned. He informed me that he had two brothers and four sisters and that they all had different names and all had favorite foods, all of which he listed. The family was new to the neighborhood and had come from a long way off up the hillside (it sounded like Upper Village). The burrow they were living in now was much nicer than the one they used to live in.

I continued with my work. By the time the sun was setting, I had finished the main chamber and had started on a second tunnel to serve as an emergency exit (there was always at least one emergency exit in every lorpa burrow).

Baxter had stayed to watch. I told him he had to go home now because it was close to getting dark. He said, "I'll be back tomorrow." Then he ran away. I thought his parents had to be very liberal-minded to let him stay out by himself for so long at such a young age.

I made my way home and went to my room, slinking around my parents, who were settling down in the main chamber. I was eager to tell Contessa that I had started digging. It was past the time of day when she was wont to come visit me with food. I couldn't visit her in *her* room. To do that would have risked setting my father off (that's how bad things were between us). So I waited. But Contessa didn't come that evening. She had already gone to sleep.

The next day, I was up at first light and on my way to the new hole. By the time the sun rose, I was pushing out dirt. Once again, Baxter showed up, only this time it was for breakfast.

"Do you have anything to eat for me?" he asked. He took up his crouching position from the day before.

"No."

"I'm hungry."

"You better go home."

He retreated a couple of steps, and I went down the hole. When I came out again, rolling a pebble, he was still there.

"I wish I had something to eat."

"You need to go home to your family."

"My sister hasn't come back yet." Presumably he meant that his sister was still out foraging.

"I can't help that."

Once more, I went down the hole. This time I stayed down a considerable while. But you could only scrape so much dirt loose before you had to move it up the tunnel. You did this by kicking it behind you as you stepped backwards. Then, when you got near the surface, you turned around and, facing forward, pushed the dirt out into the open with your face.

"I'm hungry!" I heard Baxter say.

When I got all the way out of the hole, I shook the dirt off.

"I wish there was some *food* for me to eat!"

"You are a varmint!" I told him. "All right, let's go find something." I was hungry myself.

We looked around for bugs and insects. We came upon a grasshopper nymph sunning itself on a rock, but it was too quick for me. We had better luck with some grubs, which I was able to scratch out from under a bush. Baxter gobbled them up. Grubs were the best food value as far as bugs went, but they weren't easy to find. I caught some other bugs that weren't as tasty. Fortunately, Baxter liked them all. After that, I told him I had to get back to work. Once again, Baxter took up his crouching position, and I went down the hole.

I wasn't paying much attention to him, otherwise I would have noticed that the critter was getting drowsy. It startled me when, turning around at one point, I saw that he had fallen asleep. This was a dangerous thing to do above ground, especially for a young one (a young one might not awaken when the predator alarm was sounded). I took hold of him and shook him and told him he had to go home *now* before he was picked off by a hawk.

"Get going!" I was gruff.

Baxter said he would, but that he would be back after his nap. I watched him leave.

Baxter had not returned by the time I decided to call it a day. It was only midafternoon, but I had finished the emergency-exit tunnel and had also dug out two secondary chambers to the rear of the main chamber. I wanted to get home early before there was any chance of Contessa's going to bed. I needed to tell her what I was up to.

I ran all the way. When I got to the entrance hole, she was just coming outside, pushing some loose dirt in front of her.

"Are Mom and Dad here?" I asked. I was panting from my run.

"Of course they are. They're having their nap."

"I need to talk to you."

"Make it quick. I have to go out for longbugs." The longbugs would be for my father. They were his favorite treat.

Keeping my voice down, I told her about the new burrow and explained that things had gotten so bad with Dad and myself, the way he was acting, that I was going to have to leave home and not come back.

It didn't take Contessa more than a moment to consider.

"I'm going with you!" she said.

"What! You can't do that!"

"I'm going with you!" She would not be gainsaid. "Is the new burrow ready?"

"Pretty much. More or less."

"If I stay, I'll be the only one left with Mother and Father, and I won't have that. You're the only reason I can stand living here."

She had never had a close relationship with our parents. There would be very little love lost. In any case, she was getting to be a mature female, and it was only natural that she should want to start a life of her own. But leaving home with *me* would not meet with our parents' approval—it would, in fact, send my father into a rage. The problem was that I was not a proper creature for going out into the world with: I was not a suitor. Only a suitor had the right to separate a daughter from her family. The separation meant, among other things, depriving the family of whatever contribution the daughter was making towards maintaining the household. To be sure, this factor wasn't always significant. Sometimes a daughter's contribution was negligible or even non-existent (such as Queenie's, for example, according to Dylan). In Contessa's case, the loss to the family would be considerable. Not only was she an excellent hunter and forager, but she was also a hard-working housekeeper who regularly changed the bedding and cleaned out the tunnels. She also kept the grass under control around the outside of the burrow.

"We'll leave tonight," she said, "under cover of darkness!"

Chapter 4

That night had to be one of the most nerve-racking of my life. Getting out of the burrow was not a problem—we waited till Mom and Dad were asleep and then scurried up one of the emergency-exit tunnels. In doing so, we almost certainly woke them up, but they wouldn't have attempted to come after us, not in darkness. Once we were on the outside, however, Contessa and I had to proceed very carefully. There was no moon to guide us, only starlight. In the daytime we would have run the paths. Now we crawled.

I led the way, stopping periodically to stand up on my hind legs to look and listen. The whole village was asleep, there was no doubt about that. But a different world was awake. All around, there was the hum of insects; from far away came the intermittent, strange call of some animal; and from close by came sudden, heart-stopping rustlings in the grass. A mouse was no threat, but a weasel would try to kill us. There was also the danger of getting picked off by a nighthawk or owl. There would be no alarm-chirps to warn us that a predator was in the sky.

We reached a thoroughfare called the Pike. This well-trodden path ran slantwise down the hillside and would take us all the way into Lower Village. In theory, traveling the Pike would allow us to move faster. But we would also be more exposed.

Contessa was following close behind me.

"Shouldn't we keep to the *back* ways?" she said.

I was afraid if we did, we'd get lost.

"Not in the dark. This is the only way I know."

We proceeded down the Pike as quickly as we could while still crawling. It was excruciatingly tiring. The first indication we had reached Lower Village was the gritty feel of loose dirt under our feet. This was the excavated burrow dirt that in Lower Village was habitually flung and scattered rather than built up into neat, half-ring piles. The loose dirt was everywhere. One consequence of this was that in the dark—as I now discovered—the paths leading off from the Pike were almost impossible to identify as such. Somehow, we managed.

"Well, here we are," I finally said to Contessa. You could barely see the hole in front of us. Despite the ordeal of getting there, I was highly pleased with myself. "The new burrow!"

"Go on *in*," Contessa said.

I went down the hole.

As a lorpa, you had to be on the alert for danger every moment of your life, even when you were asleep. Just because you were highly pleased with yourself for having dug your own burrow didn't mean you could let your guard down. I was so eager to get Contessa underground, so eager to show off my new home to her, that I failed to heed the warnings of my senses. My sense of smell should have stopped me well before I got into the main chamber. What happened in the main chamber was that I ran smack into a mass of warm fur. Only then did I react and run back up to the surface. Contessa hadn't even begun to follow me when I crashed into her.

"What are you doing!" she rasped at me. I had knocked her over.

"There's someone *in* there!" My heart was pounding. "What!"

But it wasn't just someone. It was a pile of sleeping children—and I knew who they were.

"It's a *family*," I said. "They've moved *in!*" Baxter—confound him!—had told me he had a total of six siblings. He had even told me their names. And now here they were, sleeping in my burrow! But where were the parents? Coming down the tunnel, I should have been met by a mouthful of sharp teeth.

"How could you let this happen?" Contessa was furious.

"I didn't *let* it happen—"

"Now where are we going to sleep? I'm cold!" A chill wind had risen. The hum of the nighttime insects had all but ceased.

"I guess we better go home," I said.

"We can never do that. Father would kill you."

She meant this literally. My father was not going to see my role in Contessa's flight from home as anything other than an act of treachery. He would, if he could get his paws on me, mete out the harshest punishment he was capable of.

I said, "We'll find an unused hole." I was thinking of one of the abandoned holes that were so numerous in Lower Village. Most were shallow, but some were deep enough to shelter in. "Come on." I started to walk away.

"How are we going to know a hole is unused?" Contessa said, following me.

This was a point. At night, it wouldn't be so easy. I could sniff from outside the hole (this is what I should have done earlier). If the hole was *occupied*, the chances were good I'd be able to tell immediately. But if I couldn't tell, that didn't necessarily mean the hole was *unoccupied*. I'd have to crawl in, sniffing as I went.

I thought of Dylan's family. Could we ask them to take us in? Hardly. Calling at someone else's burrow in the middle of the night just wasn't done. They'd think I'd gone crazy. Besides, Dylan was the only member of his family who knew Contessa, and he wouldn't even be there. We certainly couldn't go to Buddy's or Scooter's. Both my brothers had families with young children. Even if one of them consented to take us in, neither would view Contessa's flight from home any differently from the way my father was going to view it. Scooter might try to give me a thrashing then and there. Both he and Buddy were quite capable.

Turning to face my sister, I said, "We'll dig a hole ourselves. From scratch."

"From *scratch?*" If Contessa hadn't been so tired and cold, she probably would have cuffed me one. Things were not going as anticipated.

"From scratch."

The thing to do, I decided, was to find a spot farther down the hillside outside of town. The digging would be easy there, and we wouldn't run the risk of trespassing on anyone's property. I explained this to Contessa, emphasizing the easiness of the digging. She listened without objection, and we started moving again.

When we got onto the Pike, we proceeded to the edge of the village.

"Now, stay right behind me," I said.

We crossed into the wild country. This meant there were no more detectable paths. Every few steps we bumped into tufts of grass that we had to detour around. It was dizzying. The only guide we had was the slope of the hill, and even this proved deceptive. Somehow, we became separated. Contessa must have gone left when I went right or vice versa. I only discovered we were no longer together when I stopped to say something to her.

"Contessa? *Contessa?*"

I got up on my hind legs and emitted a sharp chirp. It wasn't an alarm-chirp, but a "where are you?" chirp. Contessa's response didn't come from the direction I expected. It seemed to come from down the hillside, as though she had gotten ahead of me. I set out for her but soon became muddled. I emitted another chirp. This time her response seemed to come from across the hillside, laterally. It also seemed to come from farther away. What was happening was that she was on the move searching for *me* at the same time as I was on the move searching for *her.* The only thing to do, I finally realized, was to keep up the process of call and response with very short intervals between the calls. After bumping into a lot more tufts and making a few more wrong turns, I found her.

She was crouching in the grass.

"This is as far as I go," she said.

I felt her ears. They were cold. On the spot, I cut into the ground, and the dirt began to fly. When the hole reached a certain depth, I had to start moving the loose dirt up to the surface in stages, kicking and stepping backwards. I didn't bother to push the dirt out with my face for the last stage but kept kicking with my hind legs. I don't think any lorpa ever dug more furiously than I did that night. Within a surprisingly short time, we were in possession of a modest-sized chamber at the end of a tunnel, or, rather, two tunnels, for I hadn't neglected to dig an emergency exit. Contessa moved in, and I lay down next to her with my warming body.

Chapter 5

By the time I woke up, Contessa had already risen and gone out in search of food. Outside the burrow, I took a good look around. We must have traveled some distance, because the slope of the hillside had begun to flatten. I could still see out across the plain, but, looking uphill, I couldn't see the village, even on my hind legs. This wasn't particularly to be wondered at. What was unusual was that I had no idea in which direction the village lay. In the daytime, the lorpa sense of direction was highly acute. But moving around at night was treacherous. It was like moving around with one eye poked out!

I started to busy myself scraping together as much of the loose dirt from the previous night's excavation as I could. In a short while I had created a small, half-ring pile on the uphill side of the burrow hole. I then stood by and waited for Contessa's return.

She came carrying a mouse. When she saw the half-ring pile of dirt, she dropped the mouse and ran to the pile and started kicking it apart. I thought she had lost her mind.

"If he comes *looking* for us," she said as she kicked, "your pile of dirt will tell him that the occupants of this burrow come from the Far End!"

By *he*, she meant our father.

"Why would he come looking for us?"

"So he could drag me home—after killing you."

The idea that our father (or any lorpa, for that matter) would go to that much trouble to get his runaway daughter back, unespoused though she was, seemed farfetched. My feeling was that we were perfectly safe so long as we stayed out of the Far End.

We ate the mouse in silence.

When the meal was over, Contessa said, "What's our next step?"

"Our next step?"

"What are we going to *do?*"

I hadn't thought about our next step, but it took me only a moment to figure out what it should be.

"We're going back to Lower Village," I said. "That's *my* burrow. I dug it. Those critters are going to have to clear out!"

"I don't want to go back to Lower Village." She was afraid of being seen by our father.

"Do you want to live in the wild for the rest of your life?"

Contessa knew as well as I did that living outside the village was inherently dangerous.

"I'm gonna get back my property!" I said.

We decided that Contessa would accompany me as far as the village edge and wait there while I did the work of removing Baxter's family from my burrow. When the job was done, I would rejoin her and we would enter the village together. Once she was settled in the new burrow, she would feel safe.

"The sooner we get moving, the better," I said.

We set off. Despite the lack of a trail, we made steady progress up the hillside, though neither of us knew precisely in which direction the village lay. Eventually, we came to a place where I could see the pine tree where Dylan and I used to frolic. Now I knew where we were. When we got to the tree, I told Contessa to wait there.

"Don't be long," she said.

"I won't be."

I entered the village. I did wonder how I was going to carry out the task I had assigned myself. Baxter's parents might resist. I was prepared to fight—I was in a belligerent mood, full of righteous indignation—but I didn't want to go down the burrow hole to fight. Inside the tunnel, it would be very hard to make headway against a determined defender.

I decided I would work from the outside. Accordingly, when I got to the hole, I stuck only my head in. From this position, I started to make offensive mouth-click noises. The mouth clicking was, in effect, territorial signaling on my part and was bound to get a reaction. To whichever of Baxter's parents came out of the hole, I would issue the order to vacate the premises. If it was Baxter's father, there might be a fight then and there. My preference, of course, was that the family leave peaceably,

but I could hardly count on that happening. If they simply refused to go, I would start pushing pebbles down the
hole—pebbles, sand, gravel, dirt. One way or another, I
would get my burrow back.

Someone did come out of the hole, but it wasn't who
I expected.

"Hi!" said Baxter.

"You!"

"Whatcha doing?"

"Go get your father."

"Why?"

"Because I tell you."

"Why?"

"Just *do* it."

"He's taking his nap."

"Well, wake him up!"

Baxter disappeared down the hole. Already I could
feel my resolve weakening.

Baxter soon came back up and informed me that his
father was coming. Then he went down the hole again.
When the father emerged, he moved slowly. He seemed
to hobble. I saw that he was a somewhat aged creature,
certainly older than my own father. Behind him came a
brood of little ones and what I took to be the mother of
the family. The latter was rather pretty. She didn't look
any older than myself, which surprised me. She took up a
position in the background and held on to one of the kits
by the scruff. Baxter was the last to emerge from the hole.
He came over to crouch by me.

"Welcome, stranger!" said the father in a kindly tone.

"Hello," I said.

"Are you one of our neighbors?"

"No, I'm not one of your *neighbors*—"

"We moved into this hole only yesterday—from just over yonder." He indicated a direction with a wave of his paw. "I haven't had time to *meet* any of our neighbors. My name is Menander. These are my children: Baxter—"

"I've met Baxter already."

"Indeed!" Menander gazed fondly on his son. "Baxter is our ambassador to the world! We're strangers here, you see. We came from up the hillside. Vet!"

"Yes, Father." This was the female that I had taken for the mother. Evidently the family had no mother.

"My daughter Vet," Menander said to me.

Vet regarded me with unblinking eyes.

"Where do we live now?" Menander asked her.

"We're in Lower Village, Father."

"That's right." Menander seemed to have to struggle to remember. "We came originally from—*Upper* Village. We were fortunate enough to find this abandoned hole here. So many of them are so shallow. The one we occupied when we first arrived—"

I looked at Baxter. The varmint *knew* that I had dug this hole! Probably he had led them here.

"This one's warmer!" Baxter said.

"Warmer," agreed Menander, "and drier. I wonder if you would do us the honor to stay—" He hesitated "I didn't catch your name!"

"Augie," I said.

"Father!" said Vet.

"I wonder—" Menander said again.

"You need to finish your nap," Vet said to him.

"My nap, yes. I need to finish my nap. But come back, Augie. We can have a nice chat and something to eat!"

I wished them all a good day and left.

This was astonishing. The father, Menander, hadn't exhibited any fear or aggression at the arrival of a stranger at his door, but had only been cordial and friendly. And the invitation to come back for a nice chat and something to eat seemed nothing short of incredible. This was not typical lorpa behavior. As for Baxter, maybe he was simply too young to know that moving into someone else's burrow wasn't something you could just *do* with impunity. As I made my way back to the tree where I had left Contessa, I wondered how she was going to take the news that the family occupying my burrow would be staying on.

I was spared the fury of her reaction. She wasn't at the tree. I looked around and called for her, but she had vanished. My first thought was that she had been carried off by some predator. But any predator coming this close to the village would have been spotted by sentries and the alarm would have been sounded. I had heard no alarm. Then I remembered Contessa's worry about our father. Had he come looking for her and found her? That seemed unlikely. The only remaining possibility was that she had run away.

"She lost her nerve," I said to myself.

I started down the hillside, bound for the burrow we had slept in the night before. That had to be where she had run to—or so I thought.

But when I got to the site, Contessa was nowhere to be seen.

Chapter 6

The next few days I spent standing long watches. The mound of dirt that Contessa had so furiously kicked apart

I re-formed, and I took up a position on top of it. You would have thought I was on sentry duty, and in a way I was. My eyes, however, were not scanning the scrubland for predators, but for my sister's return. Every so often I would emit a chirp-call.

When I wasn't on watch, I searched for food. Getting enough to eat was proving to be a problem. My hunting skills being what they were, anything that moved faster than a prairie ant (which was almost inedible) got away from me. Running after lizards, I settled for pill bugs. I remembered that pill bugs and fresh spring shoots were what Dylan said he was eating the last time I saw him— Dylan, who had looked so thin.

The sad truth was that I still needed someone to feed me. At home, Contessa had taken over the role that my parents had relinquished when they stopped sharing. And now, in Contessa's absence, I was in a fix. Waiting for her return, I was getting hungrier and hungrier.

By the fifth day I realized I couldn't wait forever. I would have to go find her. The question was, where to look? It seemed reasonable to suppose that she might be hiding out someplace in Lower Village. She might have sought out some abandoned hole that felt safe to her. What was needed, then, was to find that hole. Alas, Lower Village was a large neighborhood; but I would try. Both for her sake and my own, I felt I had to locate her.

The first order of business would be to stop by Menander's burrow—or rather *my* burrow, currently occupied by Menander and his seven children. Somebody in that large family might have seen Contessa (she looked like me, only smaller). I was thinking particularly of Baxter, the family's "ambassador to the world." I would make inquiries.

What the chances were of finding Contessa, I had no idea; but at least I had a plan of action. Before leaving to go up the hillside, I spent a long morning stockpiling as much spring grass as I could find—the fresh shoots, that is, not the old stalks, which were inedible. That way there would be something to eat when I got back (with or without Contessa). It wasn't until the sun was at its highest that I set out. Normally, high noon wasn't a time of day when you would expect to see many lorpas above ground. But when I entered Lower Village, I encountered a kind of gathering mob. There were maybe ten plus ten lorpas total, some old, some young, and they were standing, crawling, and hopping around. All of them seemed to be jabbering.

"What's going on?" I asked a young one.

"Prairie dogs!" the young one said.

"Prairie dogs?"

"Down on the plain!"

"You mean somebody ran into prairie dogs down on the plain?"

"Somebody did!"

"Was there a fight?"

"I don't know—but there's going to be!"

An older lorpa grabbed me by the scruff.

"We're going to *do* something!" he said. "*Get ready!*"

It took considerable effort on my part to wriggle out of his grip.

"*Get ready!*" he said again, this time with a snarl.

The young one started jumping up and down from sheer excitement.

"Get ready! Get ready! Get ready!"

Whatever was happening, I didn't want any part of it. Cautiously, I backed away. The older lorpa glared at me. I made a break and ran.

To get to Menander's, I had to cross the Pike. I didn't stop running till I reached the intersection, where I paused to look both ways. I was panting hard. The thoroughfare was clear except for two lone figures on the uphill side. Something about the way they were moving caught my attention. They were scurrying back and forth as though they couldn't make up their minds which way to go. "Prairie dogs! Prairie dogs!" one of them called out. I recognized the lorpa as Dylan's father. The other lorpa was *Queenie*. "No! No!" she cried. The sight of them amazed and confused me—especially the sight of Queenie. She was supposed to be the lazy one, and here she was, out on the Pike scurrying back and forth! Both she and her father appeared to be highly agitated. Fortunately, neither of them noticed me, and I ran on.

When I got to the entrance to Menander's burrow, I was in a state. My heart was racing, and my breath was coming so hard and fast that I almost began to chirp-call involuntarily. I called for Menander. There was no immediate response, and the thought came to me that maybe the family had moved out. Finally, to my relief, Vet's face appeared.

"What do you want?" she said, keeping her head inside the hole. It wasn't the friendliest of greetings.

"Can I talk to your father?"

"He isn't feeling well."

"I need to talk to him! I need to find out if he knows—if any of you know—anything about my sister, Contessa. You may have seen her. She's about your size but looks like me. She has light brown fur—"

"She hasn't been here."

"Maybe you've seen her around Lower Village."

"No."

"Maybe Baxter—"

"No. I'm sorry. No one here has seen her or knows anything about her."

Her words conveyed a sense of finality, as though there was nothing more to be done.

"Something's happened to her!" I almost whimpered.

Vet just looked at me.

"Would you keep an eye out? If she comes by, would you tell her I'm searching for her? I'm living down the hillside. Contessa knows where. I had to dig there because we had no place to sleep and it was dark and cold!"

"I'm sure you'll find her, Augie." Vet's tone was suddenly more sympathetic. "I'm sure she's all right."

"If you could keep an eye out."

"I will."

"And Baxter, too. He sees a lot of what goes on, doesn't he?"

"We'll all keep an eye out. If Contessa comes by, we'll tell her to go to your burrow."

"Tell her to stay there until I come back! It's down the hillside."

"Down the hillside."

"I have to keep looking for her!"

I pulled myself together and made Vet a kind of formal bow. Then I hopped away. Before going too far, I allowed myself a parting, backward glance. Vet hadn't moved. She was watching me. She must have watched me till I was out of sight.

My search for Contessa gave me a new appreciation for the back ways of Lower Village—the arbitrary twists and turns, the dead ends, the roads to nowhere. First I went one way, then another; then I would backtrack. My search would have been more efficient if I had allowed myself to use the Pike. But the Pike was where I had just seen Dylan's father and Queenie, and I had no wish to tangle with them. They wouldn't have been helpful.

No one on this side of the Pike appeared to have heard about the prairie dogs. There was no one out except the sentries. I approached one who was standing on top of a little hump. Every so often he would turn his head to scan a different part of the landscape or sky. Otherwise, he was as motionless as a stone. You weren't supposed to distract the sentries. If I had asked him if he had seen Contessa, he wouldn't have answered me. He might have cuffed me one, though,

What I did was, when I came to a hole that looked and smelled like it might be tenanted, I called down Contessa's name. Then I retreated a few steps. It did occur to me that my calls might not be welcomed by lorpas who were not my sister, and, indeed, this was invariably the case. A face would appear at the hole and scowl. One householder was good enough to tell me that there was no *Contessa* on the premises and that he had never heard of any critter going by that name. "Now go away!" Another householder jumped out of the hole and bared his teeth at me. My search finally came to an end when an especially fierce one jumped out of the hole and chased me back across the Pike! Disturbing a lorpa in his or her burrow, even in Lower Village, was a hazardous proposition.

I now found myself a good deal farther up the hillside than I was before. The fierce one had, in fact, chased me all the way to the edge of the old neighborhood. You could always tell where the Far End began, because suddenly the paths were straighter and cleaner and the grass growing around the burrows was trimmer. Most telling of all were the half-ring piles of excavated dirt built up around the uphill sides of the burrow entrances. All was quiet in the Far End. The residents were taking their rest, secure in their chambers.

And Contessa? I had to wonder. She had been mightily afraid that our father would come looking for her, that he would find her and forcibly bring her back home. Now, after my failure to locate her in Lower Village (even considering just the small part of it I had searched), that idea didn't seem so far-fetched. *Had* he brought her back?

If Contessa was with our parents, there was really nothing more for me to do except go back down the hillside. If she wanted to leave home again, she would have to leave without my assistance. But I couldn't just abandon my search for her without knowing for sure that she was there. I would have to find out somehow. It took some stiffening of my resolve. I had hoped never to have to enter the Far End again.

I set off at a slow walk.

Obviously, calling for Contessa at the burrow entrance was out of the question. If my father heard my voice or otherwise detected I was anywhere near, he'd come after me. No, what was needed was an indirect approach. Mrs. Chew and Mrs. Burgoyne were two of our neighbors who lived across the way. They each had an unobstructed view of our burrow entrance. I knew this because we had unobstructed views of their burrow entrances. All my mother had to do was stick her head out into the open a little, which she did many times a day, and she could see them. I didn't know whether Mrs. Chew and Mrs. Burgoyne were as avid as my mother was when it came to burrow watching, but my guess was that they were. For this reason, I thought there was a good chance that at least one of them would be able to tell me what I wanted to know about Contessa. Happily, neither of them was on good terms with my mother—a circumstance that made me feel I could trust them.

I chose to go to Mrs. Burgoyne because her burrow wasn't quite so frighteningly close to our own as Mrs. Chew's was (Mrs. Chew's was hardly more than ten hops away, almost directly across the path). With a thudding heart, I crouched by the entrance hole and called Mrs. Burgoyne's name. Her face appeared almost at once.

"What is it, Augie?"

"Can I come in?"

"You know I'm all alone here." Mrs. Burgoyne was a widow and had no children. "I'm not accustomed to having callers."

"Please!" I was worried about being seen by my mother.

"All right."

I crawled into the hole and followed Mrs. Burgoyne down into the main chamber. It was a comfortable house. There were great quantities of dried grass on the floor.

"Make yourself at home, why don't you," Mrs. Burgoyne said.

I lay down on the grass padding. It had a nice smell.

"Now tell me why you are in such a fever to see me."

"It's a long story."

"I'm listening."

I proceeded to tell her essentially everything that had happened since Contessa and I left home. I told her of my concern that my father may have set out to find Contessa to forcibly bring her back. When I asked her if she had seen any sign that my father had succeeded in doing this, she said no.

"And I see everything that goes on around here. You can take it from me, your sister's not at home."

"Well, thank you for the information, Mrs. Burgoyne."

"You don't have thank me, Augie."

"I guess I better be going."

It was a relief to know Contessa wasn't where she didn't want to be. But now it was back to the question of where she *was*. I had to keep searching.

"You know," said Mrs. Burgoyne, "you should stay a while. Contessa may yet come back." She gave me a bump with her nose. Mrs. Burgoyne was still a plump and attractive female. "I'll get us some food."

I was terribly hungry and let her feed me. In retrospect, it might have been better not to have taken her advice about staying a while. But I did take it and stayed the rest of the day and then overnight. The next morning, when I was set to leave, Mrs. Burgoyne said I'd better stay one more day just in case Contessa came back *that* day. So I stayed again. The morning after that, the same thing happened, and before I knew it seven days and nights had gone by.

It was a strange existence, part worry and anxiety and part domestic living and routine. Each morning, after telling me I'd better stay one more day, Mrs. Burgoyne left the burrow to go on her "errands," by which she meant her walk out onto the hillside to catch and gather that day's food. When she came back, we had something to eat and she told me where she had been and whom she had seen and any gossip she had heard. After we finished our food, she stationed herself at the burrow entrance with just her head peeping out and, while I remained below keeping myself hidden, gave me reports on what was happening at the entrance to my parents' burrow.

In this way I learned that my father went out every evening before the sun set and didn't return until it was nearly dark. Whether this meant he was searching for Contessa or just going out for food was hard to say, but it was a new development. He had never gone out in the evening before. Sometimes, earlier in the day, he would just stick his head out of the hole and sniff the air. Mrs. Burgoyne said that the number of my mother's appearances at the hole—to look out across the way—had fallen off significantly but that she seemed to be leaving the burrow more often to go foraging. These reports made me sad. My parents were having to adjust to the new conditions of their lives. They were also having to cope with the dashing of their expectations for their daughter and the treachery (as they saw it) of their son. I couldn't help feeling sorry for them. But I didn't regret what Contessa and I had done.

Finally, when darkness came, Mrs. Burgoyne and I would have our last meal of the day together and retire to bed. From the beginning, she was very affectionate and loving towards me.

But at the end of seven days Contessa hadn't returned home and no one Mrs. Burgoyne had spoken to on her morning errands could tell Mrs. Burgoyne anything concerning her whereabouts.

Chapter 7

My decision finally to leave went hard on Mrs. Burgoyne. She said I was being *precipitous*, not to say *cavalier* (two words I didn't know). I told her I had to keep looking for my sister and that lurking so close to my parents, even underground in her burrow, put me in constant danger of being discovered. She said that I didn't care about her. I said that I *did* care, that I was very grateful to her. She said she didn't want my *gratitude*. Then she ordered me out of the burrow. But before I could leave, she said "Wait!" and brought out food for me to take with me. I told her I would never forget her kindness.

"Oh, Augie!"

We nuzzled together one last time. I really did care about her, but there could be no future for us. She would never leave the Far End, and I could never live there in safety, not with my father so near. Mrs. Burgoyne stood by while I filled my cheek pouches full of minced grubs, spring grass, and mouse innards. I felt like a cad.

"Fare thee well!" she said. With my cheek pouches bulging, there wasn't much I could say, so I turned away and crawled up the entrance tunnel to the outside.

I got out of the Far End as fast as I was able and made for Menander's burrow. I wanted to inquire once more if anyone in the family had seen or heard anything about Contessa. Menander himself responded to my muffled call at the entrance hole. He told me right off, without my having to ask, that unfortunately no one in the family had anything to report.

I accepted Menander's invitation to stay for dinner. I was able to contribute, thanks to the generosity of Mrs. Burgoyne, and disgorged the contents of my cheek pouches onto the ground. The entire family came out for the feast. Vet emerged first and was followed by Baxter who was followed by the five younger kits. They all carried foodstuffs that Vet herself had no doubt spent that very morning procuring. I was glad to be able to contribute the minced grubs, spring grass, and mouse innards, which were a big hit with Baxter and the younger kits. Vet ate only from what she and her siblings had laid out, which included a number of grasshopper nymphs. Vet must have been a very good hunter. I didn't mention who was responsible for my contribution to the feast—nor did I mention that I had been living with her for the previous seven days.

Menander asked me what I knew about the prairie-dog situation. I said the only thing I knew was what I had been told when I came up the hillside looking for Contessa, that somebody reported coming across prairie dogs down on the plain.

"But you saw the excitement in the village?" Menander said.

"I did. Someone took hold of me by the scruff and told me to *get ready.*"

Menander shook his head.

"Since then," I went on, "I've been underground and haven't heard anything." During my stay with Mrs. Burgoyne, she relayed all kinds of gossip but said nothing about the prairie dogs.

Vet now spoke. She said there had been reports of burrow invasions in both Upper Village and Lower Village. The invasions had all taken place at night.

"The reason we left Upper Village," she explained, "was that a neighboring family had a break-in and barely escaped with their lives. But the break-ins are happening here, too!"

She said that no one could confirm that the prairie dogs were responsible, but they were being blamed just the same. There had been calls for action, and several "sweeps" had already taken place. These were forays down onto the plain carried out by relatively large groups of lorpas. The idea was to drive off any prairie dogs that could be found and to do it with such ferocity that no prairie dog would ever think of wandering into "our" territory again. Now there was talk of a raid on the prairie-dog village.

Menander said he was greatly concerned about the consequences of a widening war.

"A raid on their village!" I exclaimed. "I never heard of such a thing!"

"It's happened before. In my father's time—"

"Can I go on a raid, Pop?" Baxter asked. He had grown some since the last time I saw him.

"Hush!" said Vet, cuffing him one on the side of his shoulder.

"They are harmless creatures!" Menander declared.

Baxter had retreated out of Vet's range.

"I wanna go!" he cried.

This time Vet pounced. She grabbed her brother by the scruff and spanked him vigorously on his hindquarters. As soon as she was done, he ran down the burrow hole.

"Irrepressible youth!" Menander said. "You may find it hard to believe, but I was like that once." As though on cue, he began to cough and wheeze. Vet came to his aid and stroked his fur. Menander was not in good health.

When it was time to leave, Menander told me to come back again, that I would always be welcome in his home. He advised me to be careful out in the village.

"It's easy to get caught up in events. To get caught up in the excitement! Do you take my meaning?"

"I do," I said. "I certainly don't want to go to war against the prairie dogs!"

I bowed to Vet.

She said to me, "Augie, please come back. We'd love to have you."

This was a surprise.

"And it doesn't matter if you don't bring food," she added. "If you're ever hungry—"

"Bring food!" said one of the kits.

"Hush!" said Vet. "If you're ever hungry, please come by."

"It's a standing invitation!" said Menander.

I was amazed. Why were they so nice to me?

"Thank you!"

I left them and headed for the lower hillside. Perhaps, in my absence, Contessa had returned to our little burrow in the wild. But as I made my way, somehow I knew she had not.

Somebody else had been there, though. My store of spring grass was gone, and there were leavings on the floor, mostly small-animal bones. Contessa would never have left such a mess. The leavings weren't fresh, and I concluded that some creature had just stopped in to take a meal and then moved on.

I cleaned everything out and went to bed with a heavy heart. When sleep came, it brought disturbing dreams. Lorpas from the village were chasing me across the scrubland, and I didn't know why. Vet was watching from the heights. "Augie!" she was calling out. "Please come back! We'd love to have you!" I wanted to get to her, but there was no clear path. Then the wind began to howl. My pursuers were getting closer, nipping at my tail stub! Someone was making *sniffing* sounds—

Suddenly I was wide awake. The sniffing sounds weren't coming from my dream. They were coming from up the entrance tunnel. It was still nighttime—I knew this because my body told me I should still be asleep—and my first impulse was to run out of the burrow by way of the emergency exit. But that action would have been premature.

There were basically two kinds of burrow invasion. In the first kind, the invading creature came down the entrance tunnel. This could usually be defended against successfully. You knew the creature wasn't going to be bigger than you, or not much. You simply took up a position in the tunnel and bared your sharp teeth. In the tunnel, the creature would have very little maneuvering room, and eventually he would give up and go back up to the surface.

In the second kind of invasion, the creature tried to *dig* his way in. This was a much more serious threat. You knew the creature was going to be bigger than you (that was why he was digging—he was too big to come down the tunnel), and you knew he'd be able to create all the maneuvering room he needed. As soon as you heard that digging sound, you got yourself out of the burrow *fast*.

I positioned myself in the tunnel just a little way up from where it let in to the chamber. As long as I heard no digging, I would stay put, ready to bite whatever came down. Presently the sniffing sounds got louder. The creature was getting closer. Then I heard a familiar voice.

"Augie?"

It seemed incredible. I started up the tunnel. The creature beat a hasty retreat to the surface. When I came out, there was Dylan, standing in the moonlight. He was holding on to something that he had apparently just picked up off the ground, defensively, as though he wasn't quite sure who I was going to turn out to be.

"Dylan!" I exclaimed.

"Augie!" He was relieved to recognize me.

"You're alive!"

"Yup, I'm alive. It's me."

"I can't believe it! I thought you were gone forever! Where have you been all this time?"

"I've been all over!"

"All over?"

"Can we go inside?"

I went down the burrow hole and Dylan followed. He came pushing the thing he had been holding on to.

"The last time I saw you—" I began.

"Augie, I need to go to sleep right away. Can we talk in the morning?"

He had pushed the thing into the chamber. I could tell by the smell that it was the carcass of some animal, or what remained of the carcass. Dylan took his place by the chamber wall and was quiet. I couldn't imagine what he had been doing out in the middle of the night. But I would have to wait till morning to find out. All would become clear then. I settled down in my own place and tried to relax. But sleep was a long time coming. It was just too incredible—Dylan and I were together again!

Chapter 8

It was the smell of the carcass that woke me up. It had grown rather strong in the closeness of the chamber. Dylan was still asleep.

I went outside into the cool, fresh air. The sun hadn't risen yet, but the sky was getting light, and I wondered whether I shouldn't try to scare up something to eat. It was too early to look for bugs—it was much easier to find them after the sun was up—but I could gather some spring grass. I wondered where Dylan had found his carcass. He certainly couldn't have brought the animal down himself (as a hunter, he was even more ineffective than I was). It was probably the discard of some predator or high-order scavenger. I decided against going foraging and got up into the sentry position and watched the landscape brighten with the new day.

When Dylan emerged from the burrow, he came pushing the carcass in front of him. I was now able to get a good look at my friend from childhood, and what I saw was a shock. Dylan had turned into a chubby lorpa!

"Dylan!" I exclaimed. I had never seen anyone looking so well fed.

"Here's breakfast!" he said.

We set to eating the tough meat.

When we had each consumed a goodly portion, Dylan said to me, "Augie, I didn't know this was your burrow. I thought it was abandoned."

"How long have you been living here?"

"Well, I came here only a few days ago. It was just by chance. I haven't been back since, not till last night. The night before that I stayed at my place outside the Far End."

"Your place outside the Far End?"

"All my burrows are outside of town. I've been keeping away—mostly."

I wondered why anyone would have more than one burrow.

"How many burrows do you have?"

"Five—if you count this one. I move around a lot. I stay one day in one place and the next day in another." Dylan resumed nibbling on the carcass.

I had to comment: "You don't look like you've been lacking for food."

"Augie, remember when I came to see you outside your folks' burrow?"

"I do! That was the last time I saw you."

"You know what I was getting to eat? Spring grass! Maybe a few pill bugs if I got lucky."

"You were awfully thin."

"I was starving. And it didn't get any better after I left you. For days I got almost nothing. You wouldn't have known me. I started talking to myself."

"You should have come back! I would have gotten something for you."

"Where from? Not from your folks. Not for me."

"Contessa would have given you food."

Dylan liked Contessa.

"Well, let me tell you. I was getting wearier and wearier, and I began to spend more and more time in my hole in the ground sleeping. Then the point came when I just didn't care anymore and I no longer went out. I fell into a long sleep."

"The winter sleep!"

"Only it's not winter, Augie. This was where the story was going to end. But one night something happened that changed everything. I was awakened by the sound of digging. Of course, I knew what *that* meant: some critter was gonna come into the burrow and try to kill me. It was only my reflexes that saved me. In what seemed like the blink of an eye, I got out through the emergency exit and began running: *left!—right!—left!—right!*—dodging the tufts of grass. How I did it, I don't know. It was almost completely dark. Then I jumped into a tuft and listened. I could hear the critter doing his digging. Some big cat, probably. Whatever he was, he was gonna be disappointed when he found there was nothing inside my burrow he could sink his teeth into. As soon as I could, I started up the hillside. I didn't know which direction the village was. All I knew was that I wanted to put as much distance as I could between me and that critter. It was just luck that I walked into Lower Village.

"Everyone was below ground asleep. I knew I needed to get below ground myself if I didn't want to die from cold. It's strange, Augie, but the threat to my life somehow gave me strength. Suddenly I had the will to live again. I found a shallow pit where I thought digging had been abandoned, and I began to form a tunnel. But you know how it is in Lower Village: it's hard to tell what's abandoned and what's not. And, of course, it was the middle of the night. It turned out there was an entrance hole almost right next to where I was digging that I hadn't noticed. I was digging into someone else's burrow! Well, the occupants came flying out. I couldn't see them—they came out their emergency exit—but I could hear them scurry away. Then I discovered the entrance hole.

"I should have run away myself. But I started sniffing at the hole. Then I stuck my head in and sniffed some more. Then I went down into the *chamber*. What a store of food I found there, Augie! Mice, grasshoppers, grubs! Well, I started gorging myself, and when I could gorge no more, I stuffed my cheek pouches. Then I left. I spent the rest of the night in a shallow hole I dug just beyond the village edge."

"What happened to the family in the burrow?"

"They must have come back. I didn't destroy their burrow. I only *started* to dig. I stopped when I heard them running away and realized my mistake. Only it was the best mistake I ever made!"

"I'm glad you got something to eat."

"That night saved my life."

"I'm glad it saved your life."

"But don't you see, Augie? That was just the beginning!"

"The beginning?"

"The next night, the same thing happened."

"What was that?"

"I went to another burrow, only this time in Upper Village. Just as soon as I started to dig at the entrance hole, the critters came flying out of their emergency exit. It was like magic!"

I was having a hard time understanding.

"But why did you *dig* when there was already an entrance hole?"

"So I could go down and get the *food*. With no one to stop me!"

What he was saying sounded very strange.

"I tell you, Augie, there's nothing to it! You *dig*, and they *leave*. You will never go hungry again." Once more, he resumed nibbling on the carcass.

"Do you know where Contessa is?" I asked him.

"No, I don't. Why?"

"She and I left home together. We ran away at night and the next day she disappeared."

"Disappeared?"

"You might have seen her."

"Contessa!" he said wistfully. "I'm sorry, Augie, I haven't."

"We spent the night in this burrow and then went back to the village. I left her waiting at the tree while I went to do something. The tree we used to try to climb."

"I loved that tree!"

"When I came back for her, she was gone."

"I hope she isn't dead!"

Chapter 9

You had to understand that the urge to take was almost second nature with us. Given the opportunity, an aggressive young lorpa would think nothing of waylaying another lorpa who was on his way home with a piece of food in his mouth. But in such an encounter there was no guarantee that the aggressive young lorpa would come away with anything more than a bloodied brow.

Dylan was certainly not an aggressive young lorpa. Which was why his method of taking was so ingenious. There was, he explained, absolutely no risk of getting hurt, and the success rate was close to half the time. The only reason the success rate wasn't higher was that not everyone kept a store of food overnight. Some of the burrows were bare. But if one burrow was bare, there was always another to try.

The one precaution Dylan took was not to strike in the same area more than once every four or five nights. This was the reason he moved around so much and maintained multiple burrows outside the village. One night he would strike in Upper Village, say, and then transport whatever food he didn't eat on the spot to the burrow he had dug outside Upper Village. There he would sleep the rest of the night. The next night he would strike in the Far End and transport the food to another burrow, one that he had dug outside the Far End, and sleep there. Then the next night he would strike in Lower Village and transport the food to yet another burrow, one that he had dug outside Lower Village (or had taken over, if you wanted to count my burrow), and sleep *there*. And so on, all around the village. He seemed to have everything worked out—he called it a "rotation"—and was so sure of himself that I didn't like to raise objections. But there was something about taking food from someone else's burrow that felt wrong.

Dylan announced it was Knobville's turn next. Perhaps if he had selected any neighborhood other than Knobville to carry out that night's depredation in, I would have refused to go along. But he selected Knobville. The neighborhood had a strange reputation. Despite being dug through with holes, it was underpopulated. The burrows were old, and many, if not most, had caved in and were uninhabitable. Hardly any families lived there, so that there was a relatively large proportion of lorpas who were unattached, both male and female. Many of them had been ejected from their homes or had been orphaned and had moved to Knobville from other neighborhoods. I didn't know anyone from Knobville—had never even *met* anyone from Knobville—which circumstance I suspect helped me rationalize what we were doing.

We waited for the moon to come up before setting out. This was for my benefit. Amazingly, Dylan had gotten used to getting around in the dark with or without a moon. All he needed was starlight. Now he led me by moonlight up the hillside and around the outside of the village. When we reached a certain elevation, we went in. Knobville was much overgrown with grass. The plants had gotten so big and had spread out so much that almost all the burrow entrances were obscured or screened by the growth. Dylan wasn't interested in these holes. He was looking for something easily accessible.

He found it in the middle of a small clearing of bitten-down tufts. The hole was in plain sight and not obstructed by anything. I remember thinking that the entrance looked very much like what you would find in the Far End. There was even a half-ring pile of dirt built around the uphill side of the hole.

Dylan bent over the hole and sniffed.

"This one's for us," he said. The night being relatively warm, it was easy to detect the smell of occupancy. "Now, Augie, let me show you how it's done."

I stood back on my hind legs to give Dylan room.

He oughtn't to have spoken so close to the hole. For no sooner he had started to scrabble at the dirt than a creature came charging out of the hole, knocking him over. It was a horrible shock. I would have made a run for it except that, in the moonlight, I recognized who the creature was.

"You—Dylan—!" Contessa sputtered. She was breathing hard and ready to bite. She turned to me. "And you—Augie! What are you *doing* here? I can't believe this!"

I had no words. Dylan seemed to be dazed. Contessa had hit him hard.

"What are you *doing* here?" she said again. "You better clear off. Both of you!"

"Contessa!" I blurted out. "I didn't know whether you were alive or dead!"

"I'm *alive*. As you can see!"

"But—*here?*"

"I live here."

"In Knobville?"

"Yes. This is my home. Now clear off before Rory comes up!"

"Who's Rory?"

"My *husband.*"

"Husband!"

"Come back tomorrow—when it's daylight. Now get going!"

Dylan and I got going in a hurry. He went ahead of me, walking as quickly as he was able. He was walking with a limp. We hadn't yet gotten out of Knobville when he had to stop to rest. He avoided looking at me and spoke not a word. I think he was terribly humiliated. When we crossed into the wild, he didn't head back down the hillside, the way we had come, but kept going farther out into the wild. He was making for a burrow he had dug on the Knobville side of the village—one of the five he used in his rotation. It was at the same elevation as Knobville but located some distance away. When we came to within hopping range, he ran ahead and shot down the hole, leaving me to find the entrance for myself. By the time I joined him in the main chamber, he was asleep.

If Dylan felt humiliated, I felt only relief. I had just found Contessa to be not dead but alive and apparently in excellent health. It had never occurred to me that she might be living in Knobville. Our parents had always warned us to stay away from Knobville. I wondered what her husband was like. If he was like most newly attached lorpa males, he wasn't going to welcome another lorpa male dropping by for a visit to his wife, even if that lorpa male was her brother. But Contessa had said to come back when it was daylight, so maybe Rory wasn't such a bad critter.

In the morning, I asked Dylan about his leg. He said it felt better, but that was about all he said. His mood hadn't improved. This puzzled me. Of the two of us, he had always been the cheerful one, the one to bounce back after any letdown or misadventure. It did occur to me that he might not be relishing the prospect of facing Contessa again. She had said to come back when it was daylight, and Dylan regarded this summons as applying to himself as much as it did to me. Neither of us had any intention of not complying with it. Possibly he was un-happy because he had discovered that Contessa had a husband. Dylan had always been a little in awe of Con-tessa. He had always admired her. I don't think he saw himself as a serious contender for her—not in the old days, at least. But finding out she had a husband couldn't have cheered him.

We left for Knobville as soon as the sun came up. When we got to Contessa's, she was waiting for us outside the burrow hole. I could see we were in for a tongue lashing.

"You were coming to steal food!" she said.

"We didn't know you were living here—"

"You were going to drive us out of our home and steal our food!" Contessa wasn't interested in my explanations. "Don't you know you can't *do* that? You can't invade someone else's burrow! This is our village. This is *your* village! We protect one another. We don't drive one another out of our homes with fear of being killed!"

"No, I can see that now—"

"Augie, who do you think it is that warns you when a hawk is in the sky? I'll tell you who! Your neighbors!" Quietly, she began to chirp in imitation of a predator warning.

"Yes," I said, "the signal."

She kept on chirping.

"I *know* the signal."

"The dwellers of our village!" she said.

"The dwellers of our village," I agreed. "I understand. We're sorry."

"How many burrow invasions have you two carried out?"

I looked at Dylan.

"Are you aware," Contessa went on, "that the prairie dogs are being blamed for them? That we might go to *war* with the prairie dogs?"

Finally, Dylan spoke up: "Augie had nothing to do with it."

"What about last night?"

"That was my idea. Augie just came along."

"It was my first time," I said bashfully.

"I did the others by myself."

"If you really have to invade a burrow," Contessa said, "you could at least pick one that's outside our village." It seemed, then, that she wasn't categorically against the practice.

"I won't do it again," Dylan said. "I don't want to start a war with the prairie dogs."

"I would hope not!"

"Contessa," I said, "will you tell me what you did the day I left you at the tree when we came up the hillside? You were supposed to wait there for me, but when I came back you had vanished. I've been searching for you ever since."

"Oh?"

"I've been very worried."

"How long ago was that?"

"A long time."

"It does seem like an age has passed since that blessed day! I do remember waiting for you at the tree. Then Rory came by—only I didn't know his name then."

"What happened?"

"He looked at me, and I followed him home."

"Followed him home!"

"All the way to where we're standing."

"And then?"

"He looked at me again and crawled into the hole and I crawled in after him."

"I see!"

"Since then, Augie, it's been nothing but love and more love! It's one of the mysteries, like the sun and the moon. You just have to shake your head and be grateful."

"So you're happy."

"I'm happy. Look!" With her paw she indicated the bitten-down tufts of grass in the clearing. Then she hopped up on top of the half-ring pile of dirt on the up-hill side of the burrow hole. "I've relandscaped all around."

"It's very nice."

"It was a big project."

"Contessa—I wish I had learned all this earlier! Why didn't you tell me what had happened to you? I waited for you at our burrow down the hillside."

"It must have slipped my mind."

"All this time?"

"Well, Rory doesn't like me to stray very far from home. Now you and Dylan better move along. Rory went out hunting, and I don't know but that he won't be back any moment. I'd hate for him to catch you here!"

Chapter 10

Dylan and I made our way back to the edge of the village where Knobville met the farther hillside. Here Dylan stopped.

"This is the end for me," he said.

"The end? What are you talking about?"

"I'm going to starve."

"No you're not."

"I had the perfect way to get food—all the food I wanted. Now I can't do it anymore. I'm going to starve as sure as I'm alive!"

"We can manage. We can get enough to eat if we try."

"Augie, I think I'm going to have to go live by my-self."

I pictured him settling down for a long sleep in one of his burrows.

"That sounds like a bad idea."

"Are you any better at hunting and gathering than I am?"

"Yes—maybe. I don't know."

"We wouldn't make a very good team."

This judgment was undoubtedly correct.

"What I need," he said, "is to find a nice widow-lorpa to take care of me!"

He wasn't being serious.

"Dylan!" Suddenly, I was excited. "You don't know her, but there's a nice widow living across the way from my parents. Her name is Mrs. Burgoyne."

"Oh?" Dylan sounded interested.

"She's all by herself. I'm sure she would welcome a visit. Tell her you're a friend of mine. She'll give you something to eat."

"You think?"

"Yes!"

"She might not like me."

"I think she will. You'll make a good impression."

"A good impression." He proceeded to arch his back and push his fur out, making himself appear bigger than he already was. This was a trick he used to do to amuse himself. It used to amuse me, too.

"Just go to her," I said. "Tell her you're my friend. I have an idea she'll want you to stay."

"Can't we both go?"

I shook my head.

"I have to keep away from the Far End."

"Because of Contessa."

"Because I helped her leave home. If I ever run into my father—" Or either of my two brothers, I could have added. "Go to Mrs. Burgoyne. She's kind, and she's a good provider. You can learn from her." It seemed to me that if Dylan paid attention he might be able to learn some basic hunting skills from her. Not that she'd expect him to learn or even want him to. Providing food was one of the ways Mrs. Burgoyne expressed her love. But he could learn just the same.

"Shall I go now?" Dylan said.

"I don't see why not."

"You can have my burrow." It didn't sound as though he thought he'd be coming back.

"All right."

"What's going to happen to you, Augie?"

"I don't know. There's a family in Lower Village—" Up to that point, I hadn't mentioned anything about the existence of Menander's family or the burrow I had dug that they were living in. "I'll figure something out."

"Watch out for Queenie!"

"I will."

He set off back through Knobville and almost immediately disappeared into the overgrowth. I felt sure Mrs. Burgoyne would welcome him and would never want him to leave. I wondered whether I would ever see him again.

I started walking across the hillside in the direction of the burrow Dylan and I had slept in the night before. Dylan had said I could have it for my own. It was a definite improvement over the burrow down the hillside—it was deeper and roomier—but I wasn't sure I wanted it. Dylan had had a special reason for not living in the village, but I didn't. The only reason I had maintained the burrow down the hillside was that I thought Contessa might return there after her mysterious disappearance ("that blessed day"). Now that I knew she was living in

Knobville with a husband, there was no need to keep that burrow going. I could move into the village. I could move into Knobville. Why not?

Still, Dylan's burrow was perfectly serviceable and would do for the time being. When I got to the entrance hole, I realized I was hungry. By lucky chance, I found some grubs not far away. After I was finished with them, I began to drift into a kind of torpor. It was a pleasant feeling, especially in the warm sun, but I got myself below ground before there was any risk of my nodding off. And there, in the main chamber of Dylan's burrow, I began to think about Menander and his family. I wondered whether Vet would welcome a renewal of our acquaintance. Both she and Menander had invited me to come back and visit them. Vet said I didn't even have to bring food. But I rejected the idea of visiting them empty handed and hungry. If only I weren't such a poor hunter! To procure adequate food—it seemed like such a simple thing. But it wasn't. It was an everlasting challenge. I fell asleep.

As the days passed, I settled into Dylan's burrow as though I meant to stay. I had a routine: In the morning, I would gather what food I was able to; then around noon I would eat it; then after that, I would nap. The nap helped ward off hunger later in the day. One morning I surprised myself by catching a grasshopper nymph. I had never done that before and felt it was a great achievement. Unfortunately, I wasn't able to repeat the feat. More significant was my discovery of the trick to identifying stick insects. Admittedly, stick insects weren't the tastiest of creatures, but most of them were edible. I don't know whether it was this addition to my diet or the institution of the naps, but I began to think it might be possible, after all, to survive indefinitely without having to rely on someone to feed me.

It was about the sixth or seventh day after my move-in that my nap was cut short by the most extraordinary disturbance. What awoke me was the sound of chirping— "Chirp! Chirp! Chirp! Chirp!" The chirping seemed to come from many voices. Was it a warning that a hawk was in the sky? That could hardly be. These were not alarm-chirps. And why were they being produced out *here*, so far from the village? I scurried up the tunnel and poked my head out of the hole. Then I climbed out all the way and stood up to my full height.

All around there were lorpas on the move. There must have been tens and tens and tens of them. Spread out in three snake-like columns, they were coming from the direction of the village. "Chirp! Chirp! Chirp! Chirp!" they went. What were they doing? As they filed past, it seemed as though they were in a kind of trance. They took no notice of me.

Then suddenly I knew: the war had started! This was a strike force, and it was headed for the prairie-dog village. This realization ought to have filled me with dismay, but it didn't. I felt only a kind of thrill. Menander had warned me about this. "It's easy to get caught up in events," he had said. "To get caught up in the excitement!" And so it happened: I fell in with one of the lorpa columns and started to chirp myself! "Chirp! Chirp! Chirp! Chirp!" I was going to fight the prairie dogs— creatures that Menander had described as *harmless*.

The prairie-dog village was a fair march, but not as far away as I had imagined. We had to proceed across the hillside and eventually over the crest and down into a hollow. The village was on the other side of the hollow, on a gently inclined slope. It was almost completely denuded of vegetation, and just as soon as we came over the crest of the hill, we could see the burrow holes. The prairie-dog sentry could see us, too, and he immediately sounded the alarm. As the prairie dogs made for their holes, we quickened our pace, some of us hopping, some of us running, in an attempt to catch the prairie dogs above ground. But well before the first of our number got into the village, they were secure in their burrows. It now became a question of going down the holes after them. Not everyone was up to this. It was much easier to run around shrieking at the surface.

The fact was that, for all their timidity, prairie dogs were tough animals. A face-off at the bottom of one of their entrance tunnels was not likely to go in favor of the lorpa. Most of the lorpas who went down the holes came right back up. Only a few showed signs that they had engaged with the enemy. They came up scratched and bloodied. As for myself, I kept to the surface. It wasn't that I was free from the urge to create mayhem: I was running around and shrieking as loud as anyone. I just didn't see the point of risking injury for what was essentially a demonstration of force. Despite all the frenzy, no one on the lorpa side really expected to deliver a death blow to the prairie dogs. They were too tough and too well protected. We were simply harassing them. We were showing them that we were a force to be reckoned with, that we must be respected and feared.

The shrieking and running around was beginning to subside a little (we were getting tired) when I came across one of our casualties. The lorpa was a juvenile, and he appeared to be in a state of shock. His eyes were open, and he was crouching right in the middle of the action, exposed on all sides. It was Baxter.

"What are you doing here!" I said to him. "Baxter!"

He didn't seem to hear me. I wondered whether he hadn't been trampled. Perhaps he was just terrified.

I attempted to shield his head with the side of my body. Then I turned to him.

"Baxter! This is Augie! Will you do what I tell you?"

He moved forward slightly.

"Climb onto me!" I turned around and flattened myself. Baxter clambered up and dug his claws in. "Good! Now, hold on!"

I got us away from the field of battle as fast as I could, retreating across the hollow and up the overlooking hill. On the top of the hill, I stopped to catch my breath. "Baxter, how are you doing?" He made no reply to this question. Clearly, he was in no condition to get down off me. His body felt cool. Fortunately, my own body was giving off plenty of heat. Hiking him farther up my back—Baxter obliged me by digging his claws in again—I started moving at a slow, steady pace. It was, I realized, going to be a long walk back to Lower Village.

We hadn't gotten very far when the returning lorpas caught up with us. The engagement with the prairie dogs had evidently been carried off satisfactorily (indeed, the hostilities were over: there would be no more calls for action). Now, after all the mayhem, the lorpas were strangely quiet. As they passed us, I spotted Queenie and her father trudging along. I hadn't noticed them before. If they recognized me, they gave no sign. I found out later that almost the entire strike force had been made up of lorpas recruited from Lower Village.

I had been thinking that when Baxter and I got to Dylan's burrow, we could stop in there and I could go out and search for something to eat. But it occurred to me that if Baxter was left alone in his present state for very long, even underground and with bedding heaped over him, he might get too cold. No—I had to keep going. I had to get Baxter to Menander's as quickly as possible so that Vet could take charge of him. She would have food in the burrow.

"Food in the burrow!" I said to myself.

Unfortunately, my pace was slowing and I was stopping more frequently to rest. There was no helping it. The longer I carried Baxter, the heavier he seemed to get. When I finally stumbled into Knobville, the sun had set and I was near faint with exhaustion. We still had to get to Lower Village. The darkening landscape made it hard to guess the best way to proceed. I was sure I could find my way to Contessa's. Contessa could help us. She might not welcome another visit, but she could at least provide directions to the Pike. The danger was that we might not get Contessa, but Rory. That, I figured, was a chance we'd just have to take. Once more, I hiked Baxter farther up my back.

I found the clearing of bitten-down tufts and went to the hole.

"Contessa!" I called down.

Quick as ever, her face appeared.

"Augie!" she said. She came all the way out of the hole.

"Contessa, I have to take this critter home right away. Can you tell me the fastest way to get to Lower Village?"

"Of course I can." She was looking at Baxter. "Who is he?"

"His name is Baxter. He's the son of Menander. Menander is the father of the family that moved into the burrow I dug."

"The family that took it *over*, you mean?"

"They're a very nice family—"

"Did you remove them?"

"As a matter of fact, I didn't. They don't have a mother. But there's a grown-up daughter that takes care of them all—"

"You must really love her." She took a closer look at Baxter. "Do you want me to get something for him?"

I didn't have to answer. She disappeared down the hole.

"We're going to have some food for you now," I said to Baxter, hoping the mention of food would get a response. It did.

"I'm hungry," he said.

"Just you wait."

Contessa came back with her cheek pouches full of edibles. She had me flatten myself so she could feed Baxter herself. When she was done with him, she deposited some food on the ground for me, in front of my nose.

"Eat!" she commanded.

The food was most welcome, and I gobbled it up.

"That—" I began. But whatever it was I was going to say died on my lips. For behind Contessa, just inside the burrow hole, there appeared a face, the lines of which did not bode well. They were moving from surprise to hostility to anger to rage. A massive head emerged from the hole.

Contessa saw my reaction and turned around in a single jump.

"*You get back down that hole!*"

Rory gave her a startled look and got back down the hole. Contessa returned her attention to me. "You better go."

She gave me directions for getting to the Pike, and I thanked her. She told me to come see her again, but not too soon.

The wind had started to blow. A black cloud began to roll over the sky, and with the daylight already waning, Baxter and I were soon enveloped in near darkness. When we got to the Pike, I picked my way along the well-worn path with care, moving more slowly than ever. And then the cloud burst and the rain came pouring down. I could barely see anything. "Hold on!" I shrieked at Baxter, and I started to *run*.

Where I got the strength from, I don't know. Somehow, we made it to Menander's without mishap. At the entrance hole I called Menander's name over and over. The rain had turned to hail, and we were getting pelted. I remember that Vet came out and took Baxter off my back and pushed him into the hole. Then she started to push me in. I was shivering with cold. The next thing I knew, I was in a chamber padded with fragrant, dry grass. Somebody (I thought it was Menander) put some grubs down in front of me. I ate them up and lay on my side. Still shivering, I soon became conscious of the soft, warm underside of a body—a female body—being pressed up against me. It was Vet. The kits came into the chamber and piled on top of us. Somewhere in the mix was Baxter, getting the same warming treatment as I. Gradually, my shivering subsided, and I fell into a deep, dreamless sleep.

Chapter 11

When I woke up, I at first didn't know where I was. I only knew I wasn't in Dylan's burrow. Then, slowly, the events of the previous day came back to me. I was in Vet's bedroom! It was hard to believe.

Vet and the kits were gone. Only Baxter and I remained. He was sound asleep. I crawled into the main chamber, expecting to find Menander there. He was gone, too. I scrambled up the tunnel to the surface. My legs ached terribly.

"Vet!" I croaked.

She was standing not far away, next to a scrubby bush. The kits were playing in the surrounding dirt. She turned to look at me.

I hopped unsteadily to where she was and stood up.

"Baxter—" I was out of breath.

"Is he still asleep?" she said.

"Yes."

"He's going to be all right, Augie."

"Yes. And thank you—for *me*—" I wanted to thank her for taking me in.

"There's nothing I wouldn't do for you, Augie. I owe the life of my brother to you." It was a lovely thing to say. But she was sad.

"Are you well?" I said.

She didn't answer this question. She wanted to know about Baxter.

"Where did you find him?"

"At the prairie-dog village."

"I wondered. He ran away from us, you know."

"I thought so."

"He had no right. But some of the lorpas came marching past yesterday. Baxter was supposed to be taking his nap! Later, when I couldn't find him, I knew he must have run after them."

I shook my head.

"The same thing happened to *me*. I was taking my nap! Then the lorpas came marching past, and I joined up with them. They were chirping: 'Chirp! Chirp! Chirp! Chirp!' Then *I* started to chirp—"

"What happened at the prairie-dog village?"

"Well, it was a raid. There was a lot of running back and forth and shrieking. The prairie dogs had retreated into their holes. There really wasn't much we could do to get them out—we just did a lot of running back and forth and shrieking. I think what happened was that Baxter got trampled. By our own side."

"You carried him back!"

"I did." My whole body ached. I looked around for Menander. "Does your father know—about the raid?"

"Augie—he's gone away."

"What do you mean?"

"It was two nights ago. I heard him crawl up the tunnel!"

This was often the way it happened. A dying lorpa would leave during the night so he could be by himself when the end came.

"In the morning," Vet continued, "Baxter saw that he was gone and wanted to go find him. I told him he mustn't. He thought Father had gone out foraging!"

"I'm awfully sorry," I said.

"I knew it was coming. I knew it for a long time. He was never the same after Mother died."

"You took good care of him."

"Mother was so young and strong. But he was already old."

"He was old."

"Still, I can't help but grieve. I think that's why Baxter ran away. I had to explain to him what happened to his father!"

The kits were still playing around the bush.

"What about the kits?"

"Oh, Augie—I haven't told them!" She was looking at me with her sad and beautiful eyes. "Did you ever find your sister?" she said.

"Contessa is living with her *husband* in Knobville. It seems that the day she went missing was the day she and her husband met. She was supposed to be waiting for me by the tree outside the village. But he happened to come along and she followed him home."

"Sometimes a lorpa can make up her mind quickly."

"That was also the day I met you and Menander for the first time."

"I remember!"

"I hate to tell you the reason I went to see you."

"You were going to make us leave our burrow—I mean, *your* burrow."

"How did you know?"

"After you left, Baxter told me you had dug it. It was then I knew that you had come to evict us."

"Did your father know?"

"We never told him."

I was grateful for that.

"He didn't know you had come to evict us," she said, "and he didn't know you changed your mind and let us stay."

"I was more than happy to let you stay."

"He was fond of you, Augie, just *meeting* you."

I remembered being struck by that at the time. Menander had been friendly towards me—a total stranger—for no apparent reason.

"I can't understand why," I said.

"He liked the look of you."

"I liked him, too!"

"He was never wrong about these things."

Abruptly, she turned her back to me and resumed watching the kits. They had temporarily formed themselves into a heap at the base of the bush.

"The kits," I said, "they're still so young!"

"They are," Vet acknowledged.

"And now they have no father."

"No father."

"So young," I repeated. "And no father." I was dithering.

Vet didn't reply. She seemed to have gone rigid.

I moved to where I could see her face. She was looking at the critters with a fixed stare.

"If you want," I said, "*I* can be their father."

The poor thing had to close her eyes.

"But not *your* father," I emphasized.

She shook her head.

"You're my beloved!"

I almost jumped at the words. I moved closer and took hold of her front paws. She was trembling.

"Ever since the day"—she looked at me now—"when you came back to us searching for your sister! The day my life began!"

I moved one of my paws against her beating heart.

"The feast day!" I said. I thought she meant the day I came from Mrs. Burgoyne. I had come with foodstuffs then—but only because Mrs. Burgoyne had provided me with them.

"Before that! When I spoke to you alone at the burrow hole and you were so pitiful and said you had to dig down the hillside because you and Contessa had no place to sleep and it was dark and cold!"

"I had no idea!"

She leaned her head into my shoulder.

"That was the day," she said.

"I never would have believed it possible!"

"Why?"

"Because—I was nothing. I had nothing."

"Except my heart!"

"I couldn't even hunt. Not even a lizard."

"*I'll* do the hunting! *I'll* get the lizards!"

"But I'm getting better! I can catch stick insects!"

"Augie—" I could feel her breath on my fur. "You do love me, don't you?"

"Of course I do."

"Then tell me!"

"Tell you?"

"Because if you don't love me, you'll have to go away and never come back!"

"Vet—I love you! I love your family!"

"*Our* family," she said.

"*Our* family," I said.

She lifted her head up and let me nuzzle with her.

ABOUT THE AUTHOR

Kennett Lehmann lives in St. Louis, Missouri, U.S.A. In addition to *Out of the Burrow*, he is the author of the novel *Very Little Soap*.